Harriet Beecher Stowe, And others

Six of One by Half a Dozen of the Other

An Every Day Novel

Harriet Beecher Stowe, And others

Six of One by Half a Dozen of the Other
An Every Day Novel

ISBN/EAN: 9783337038991

Printed in Europe, USA, Canada, Australia, Japan

Cover: Foto ©Andreas Hilbeck / pixelio.de

More available books at **www.hansebooks.com**

Six of One

BY

Half a Dozen of the Other.

An Every Day Novel.

BY

Harriet Beecher Stowe,
Adeline D. T. Whitney,
Lucretia P. Hale,
Frederic W. Loring,
Frederic B. Perkins,
Edward E. Hale.

BOSTON:
ROBERTS BROTHERS.
1872.

SIX PREFACES.

FIRST PREFACE.

THE history of this composition is precisely told in the November number of OLD AND NEW, in which it was first announced to the public.

"What is this," said Anna Haliburton, "about a new serial in OLD AND NEW? ' *Six of One by Half a Dozen of the Other*,' — is that the name?"

The Editor of OLD AND NEW was not present; but Colonel Ingham answered for him, as, at a pinch, he does sometimes.

"What you saw was one of the unconscious prophecies which give the world a hint of its best blessings in advance."

"Would it please you, dear *padre*, to abandon the method of the pulpit for a moment, and, in somewhat clearer language, to tell us what our chief does intend, in an enterprise in which he has not enlisted our endeavors?"

"He has not enlisted you," said Ingham, "because, as it is, the Editor has enlisted our five best home story-writers, — Mr. McDonald being, alas! too far away, to unite their forces, — and it being, alas! evident that even in our seventeen hundred annual pages we cannot print a whole novel by each of them, and at the same time take care of all the world of literature, art, and religion beside."

"Once more," said Felix Carter again, "will you please to abandon the method of the bar, and state explicitly what the chief proposes?"

"He proposes this," said Ingham. "It is impossible, as I said when I was interrupted, to print a serial novel by Mrs. Stowe, and one by Mr. Loring, and one by Mrs. Whitney, and one by Mr. Perkins, and one by Miss Hale, in the same volume which contains 'The Vicar's Daughter,' and 'Ups and Downs.' The Editor sees this impossibility, and so do the distinguished writers I have named. Yet the readers of OLD AND NEW are to be considered also, — considered, indeed, first of all. And what has been determined on, in a high council of these writers of fiction, is that they, adding Mr. Hale to their number, shall unite in writing one novel, which will be a serial, and in which our readers will be able to enjoy them all together. Wishing a name which should give an idea of the method of the book, the chief consulted the Nomenclator; and the Nomenclator said the new serial should be called

'SIX OF ONE BY HALF A DOZEN OF THE OTHER.'"

"And will you tell us how the plot is constructed?"

"No; nor will I tell you the plot. All I know is, that it grew, novel and plot, much as I remember to have seen Signor Blitz's plates start from the table when he was spinning them. He announced that he would spin six earthen dinner-plates at one time. He began with one, spinning it as you spin a penny for a child; when that was well going, he started number two; and then, from a side-table started the third. If he saw one faint and weary he encouraged it by a touch of his finger at the point of revolution; and when these three were happily gyrating, like so many interior planets, he let loose in succession numbers four, five, and six. I think the chief started the novel in much the same way. He spoke to Mrs. Stowe first, and consulted Mr. Loring. Then he went to Mrs. Whitney, and sent a brief of the plot to Miss Hale. The four principals had what the Friends call 'a solid sitting;' and in the equally happy phráse of those charming people they were 'baptized into each other's spirit.' They possessed themselves mutually of the best plot, the best moral, the locale, and the atmosphere of the story. They selected the names, — actually changed Mary Yates into Rachel Holley, after Mary had been tried and found wanting. Meanwhile, our philosophical Devil-Puzzling friend, Mr. Perkins, had come cordially into the combination, so that the story is to have the benefit of his universal information, and, I suppose, of his conferences with Apollo Lyon, Esq. Thus it is that we are to publish the first chapter of ' Six of One' in December."

"Whose chapter is that?" said everybody, even the sluggish gentlemen taking out their cigars for the inquiry.

"I have told you that it is everybody's chapter."

"Do you mean to say," said Haliburton, "that Mr. Hale locked all these people up, as if he were Ptolemy Philadelphus with the seventy translators, — that he shut them into five cells in the attic of 143 Washington Street, and himself retired into a sixth, and that at the end of six months they all came out, a little haggard, bearing six manuscripts, which on examination by Rand & Avery's proof-reader, proved to be identical, even to the use of semicolons instead of comma-dashes?"

This was a very long sentence for Haliburton, or for anybody.

Ingham said that he did not mean so. But he meant that the high contracting powers had come to no dead-locks in the management of the story. "The public will undoubtedly know better than the authors themselves do who wrote what or who contributed which. All I know is, that we are to have the critical period of the life of Six of Them by Half a Dozen of the Others."

The plan having been once suggested, copies of the following sketch of a plot were submitted to each of the six contributors: —

SIX OF THEM BY SIX OF US.

Chapters I. and II.

John Bryant and Jane Gaylord grew up in District No. 1 of Marston, went to the same school, of course, &c., &c. Henry Eyre and Henrietta Silva grew up in District No. 2, &c., &c. Mark Hinsdale and Mary Yates grew up in District No. 3, &c., &c.

In all dances, frolics, sleigh-rides, &c., they paired off as above. The town supposed they were mated for life. Perhaps they supposed so themselves. But

Chapters III. and IV.

John Bryant went to Boston,
Henry Eyre to Norwich, and
Mark Hinsdale to New York to try their fortunes.
Henrietta Silva went to Boston,
Mary Yates to Norwich, and
Jane Gaylord to New York.

The law of "propinquities" affected them. The letter-writers of Marston concluded, perhaps they concluded themselves, that the old cast of parts had not been the right one, and that other destinies were over them, mating them again by residence; when   .

Chapter V.

Jane Gaylord being appointed teacher in a Chicago School, Henrietta Silva detained there in travelling, and Mary Yates on a visit there, it proved

Chapter VI.

That the fore-ordained mates were:
John and Mary.
Henry and Jane.
Mark and Henrietta.   And so the story ends.

Mem. — Note as an *aide-mémoire*, — that the original initials are J. and J., H. and H., M. and M.

It is impossible to say whether the plan would ever have gone further, but that our dear friend Mr. Frederic Wadsworth Loring, who had enlisted joyfully in the scheme, and with fun ever new descanted on it, took it into his charge and keeping. No one who talked with him about it could resist him. He compelled the authors to their duty; and soon after he left Boston for that expedition to the Pacific slope which terminated so fatally,[1] they had their first "solid sitting," four out of the remaining five being present.

The ladies protested against the names. After great canvassing, they agreed on the respective characters to be maintained by the heroes and heroines. New names were then selected to match these characters, and the briefs were altered thus : —

1. JEFF FLEMING, *dashing fellow, go ahead ;* begins with JANE BURGESS, *she a pattern.* He ends with RACHEL HOLLEY.

2. HORACE VANZANDT, *inventor*, begins with HENRIETTA SYLVA, called NETTIE, *attractive but coquettish ;* but ends with JANE BURGESS.

3. MARK HINSDALE, *bookish, and given to clouds and scenery;* begins with RACHEL HOLLEY, *regular beauty and good;* ends with NETTIE SYLVA.

MEM. — They are to be common-place, not very high-flying, people.

On this agreement the four selected their parts, Mr. Loring's was assigned to him, and absent author num-

---

[1] Mr. Loring was killed by a body of outlaws, supposed to be Apache Indians, on his return toward San Francisco, from a summer of adventure with Lieutenant Wheeler's survey.

ber six took Hobson's choice. It was tacitly agreed
(by the Editor) that each of the partners should be
entirely and personally responsible for all the imagin-
ings, opinions, and statements of all the other partners.

Only a part of Mr. Loring's work was finished by
him; and the other authors have, with a sad interest,
completed the unfinished sketches received from him.

One and another meeting has since been held, and
the result is before the readers, the original name
having been changed by the distinguished Nomenclator
of OLD AND NEW to

SIX OF ONE

BY HALF A DOZEN OF THE OTHER.

———◆———

SECOND PREFACE.

UNQUESTIONABLY the tap-root of American growth,
whether it be palmetto or pine, is of the shortest.
You transplant it very easily. And why not? The
Americans have ample room and verge enough. Our
English friends may naturally think that "home" is a
place where the inmates *stay*, and twirl industriously
round, like squirrels inside of their trundling tin domi-
cile. Not but what the Englishman travels to every
part of the world, and takes his home-comforts with
him, enjoys his sponging bath on his way to the Albert

N'yanza, and his ale in the Himalaya. But he always finds it necessary to send his children and wife "home" every year or two, to pick up the English constitution in climate, and the English "accent" in education. Our American on the other hand, wandering over the extent of our great continent, has no occult tie that fetches him back to live in the home of his childhood. His home is where his business is, where he can make his fortune. He begins his career a stern Northerner, with a theory that life is nothing but work, and by and by he turns up a lazy Southerner, smoking his pipe all day on the open veranda. From a quiet country home, he passes through college life, breasts the passions of one of our great cities, then calms off on a western farm. But do not think that you have him rooted there. If he has a good offer for his wheat-fields, he has no particular reason for holding on to them, and you may see him next in South America, or setting up a chocolate mill in New England.

Perhaps toward the end of life some sentiment leads him to take his grandchildren to look at his native village. He talks to them of its quiet, of the old homestead with broad roof sloping to the ground, with the grass coming up to the front door, and a red rose-bush against the old stone-wall, and the stream rippling behind the house. But, alas! at the end of his pilgrimage, he finds a row of tenements set up across the front-door yard, the old homestead is an Irish shanty, and a grimy factory makes a hideous noise by the side of the "quiet stream." The old man sighs with regret;

not for the calm scenes of his youth, indeed, "but" he
says, "if I had only held on to the land, what a fortune
I might have made!"

Yet is there not a matter of education in this? We
cannot boast of a strong American physical constitution, equal to that of the Englishman, but in the
facility with which the American adapts himself to the
various climates and soils in which he places himself,
does he not gain a largeness of character, a liberality
of spirit, and freedom of soul?

Our young American people find out how to centre
all their home interests in any spot where they live,
in country or city, on the farm or the plantation.
When the time comes in which they must choose their
places in life, they are not detained by considering if it
is within the circle of their birthplace. They live
where their life is. For them it is, —

"Six of One, and Half a Dozen of the Other."

———◆———

THIRD PREFACE.

A piece of a preface? Very well; with all my heart.
Though why preface, as Dickens would say, I'm sure
I don't know; seeing that prefaces are always post-
scripts.

Are there to be five prefaces? or one, conglomerate
like the story of five paragraphs? Shall we put in

"the wit of the staircase," — the things we might have said and didn't? Shall we supplement, or explain, or excuse, or gently deprecate, or mystify? And shall we do it all together, or one at a time, dividing round again? The Colonel has sent no special orders; he has, in fact, gone off the field, leaving his regiment to manœuvre for itself in this final charge upon the public, in any pell-mell fashion that it may devise. But then that shows only the great and merited confidence he reposes in us.

Well, the dear critics know all the joints in our armor: we told them at the outset where to look for them. To glance off to a different simile suggested by the word, — the ribs of the roast are all cracked beforehand: they will be poor carvers if they can't cut us up.

But that is not the metaphor that will carry me through either.

There were six balls to wind; there were six pairs of hands set to do the work. I will not pause upon that "were;" this is not the place, nor is this light preface in the vein, for speaking of how we were left to be only five.

But what wonder if, with one or two ends of our yarn out on the Highlands, one in Boston, one in Cambridge, and trailing off thence to Florida, and the other — where not? the threads should get curiously mixed and crossed and tangled, not to say broken in the process? If we have tied clumsy weaver's knots anywhere, — if we have changed and twisted more than you expected or than seemed reasonable, — before you say hastily, "That's what comes of patchwork; of course it would be a disjointed, distracted medley;" look around you at the real live threads that twist and cross and snarl and break, and are tied in the wrong places, and coming unfastened all the time in this per-plexed and jumbled world, and see if you can trace any one of them, that you discern the most of, further on a clear, uncomplicated line than you can these of ours?

I find I have done the "gentle deprecation" busi-ness, though I did not know I should when I began: if I could, without trespassing on my neighbor's divi-sion, I should just say one thing more. You need not come down upon us with the conclusion that we have not known at all, from one hand — or head — to the other, what it was to be about; how drift and turn, or how fall out. There, too, is a deep moral, and a subtle correspondence.

Somebody who set us to work *did* know, and it has all ended precisely as it was meant to do. There has been rough-hewing, but there has been shaping also, and a clear intent.

But it is not my province to "explain;" I pass the pen — to whom? Will *you* take it, queen of the clever chessmen?

FOURTH PREFACE.

It must of course be difficult for one who thinks seriously, to put forth even a story without embodying some moral truth in it. The thoughts turn so easily to inner meanings; we ask ourselves so constantly what is the real significance, the real value, the real importance of souls or emotions or persons or things or actions, — or of the whole universe, — that a story which is only a story seems very unsubstantial. Thus, the careful reader will not find it difficult to analyze six types of character in the three heroes and three heroines of this book; and if such reader love mystical numbers, Mrs. Worboise will make up the Semitic seven. Nor will it demand too much meditation to unravel the trains of thought and emotion which moved our little company of personages; nor to detect the single practical lesson which the story teaches, — one so obvious, indeed, that it may as well be stated plainly, for it is greatly needed in this dear country of ours. It is, that engagements to marry should not be carelessly made, lest youth and love be wasted in three when one is enough. And when they are made, they should be quickly ended by marriage.

FIFTH PREFACE.

THIS story offers six numbers by as many different authors. Is there nothing to choose between the six?

Some voices answer, "Indeed there is!" Already the admirers of "Uncle Tom's Cabin," have pointed out their favorite chapters. The enthusiasts for Leslie Goldthwaite know well their own, and Fred Ingham can no longer humbug his readers.

Six planned to write these few chapters for the amusement of the public. But one has been called to a higher destiny, leaving behind some fragrant traces of his memory.

But there are six principal characters. The title of the book may have something to do with them. It seems to have been indifferent which either of them chose to marry.

Gentle public, decide it either way: to us, it is

"SIX OF ONE AND HALF A DOZEN OF THE OTHER."

SIXTH PREFACE.

THE original brief of the plot of this story was drawn early in the summer of 1871. The "stage direction" was simply that the parties should meet at Chicago in the autumn of that year, to find their destiny. Little

did the innocent augurs and gypsy-women who foretold this fate for heroes and heroines know then in
what tempest of fire that destiny would be fulfilled.
Doubtful as they were — as any augur must be — of the
way in which life shall solve the mystery of life, all
that the story-tellers could do was to let the characters
grow as the conditions of their being permitted, — let
them come and go as these conditions directed, — and
leave the issue to that decision which may always be
trusted, when youth, faithful and loyal, determines for
itself what is right, and abandons the proprieties and
etiquettes suggested by Mrs. Grundy. To their dis-
may, when the 9th of October came, a conflagration
such as never will be described, devastated the beautiful
city which had been chosen for the scene where their
little story should end. This conflagration took place
at the moment these young people were there. Born
and cradled and trained to do their duty, if they could
find it, Jeff Fleming, Horace Vanzandt, and Mark
Hinsdale did not shrink from duty in the horrors of
that dreadful night and day, — and Jane Burgess, Henrietta Sylva, and Rachel Holley were as true to theirs.
It was in the midst of duty well done, in the catastrophe
of unexpected calamity, that, as the augurs and gypsy-
women had ignorantly predicted, the story ended, and
they met their destiny.

SIX OF ONE

HALF A DOZEN OF THE OTHER.

CHAPTER I.

THE snow was falling over the roofs and houses of Greyford, not in great loose feathers, but with that fine, steady, continuous descent which indicates a steady purpose.

"We are in for it now," said Dr. Sylva, as he drew on his gloves for a long ride in the neighborhood. "Nettie, here comes the snow you've been wanting."

Nettie's first movement was in the direction of the window; her second, after satisfying herself of the state of things out of doors, was — shall we tell the secret? — to the looking-glass that hung over the table in the family keeping-room. Her father had gone out, and Nettie was alone.

She stood before it considering the image therein attentively, and nodding to it with a little knowing twinkle in her eye, as if she should say, There are a pair of us, and we'll have it all our own way now.

1   A

We by no means desire to tell tales out of school, or to produce the impression that young ladies when left alone in family "keeping-rooms" are in the habit of standing before the domestic looking-glass and contemplating their own charms. All we have to remark on the present occasion is, that if Nettie Sylva was so employed, she could not easily in that house have found any thing better worth looking at.

For "the keeping-room" of Dr. Sylva was evidently as commonplace and fluffy and uninteresting a scene as family keeping-rooms of economical people who live on small incomes are apt to become. There was a faded carpet, a worn settee which served the purpose of a sofa, a book-case with Rollin's History, Hume's "History of England," Scott's Family Bible, Doddridge's "Rise and Progress," and "The Pilgrim's Progress" for reading. There was a turn-down shelf with pigeon-holes, where Dr. Sylva kept account-books and letters; there was a half-dozen of slippery hard-wood-bottomed chairs; there was a tall old clock tick-tacking in the corner; and there were rustling paper window-shades, which Nettie detested. Nettie, in fact, detested the whole room, as a horrid, poor, commonplace, dusty, musty affair. Young ladies do sometimes have just such feelings as this about the family sitting-room.

Under these circumstances, could you look over Nettie's shoulder into the looking-glass, you would feel the force of what we have been saying: that the image she saw there was the best worth looking at of any thing in the room. It isn't saying much, to be sure. Nettie Sylva was a tall, lithe, handsome girl, and looked as if she had been got up by Mother Nature in a more generous mood of mind than she generally is in when she makes our pure, delicate, spare, lady-like New-England girls. She was like a tropical flower; every thing about her was bright and rich and abundant. She had lovely golden brown hair, and ever so much of it. Her cheeks had the high bloom and color of the pomegranate. She had great, rich, velvet dark eyes with long lashes; her waist was round as an apple, and she had a beautiful fulness of form, not a common attribute of American beauty. Nettie was of very good taste, and rather liked her own looks. It was said there was a tinge of Italian blood in her veins, through some grandmother on the maternal side; but Nettie was enough of a Yankee for all that to have a pretty good sense of what things were worth, and what could be done with them practically. Consequently the store of charms which she saw reflected in the looking-glass were something that she very well knew the use of, although the use she made of them just about these days, was one that will certainly not meet the approbation of the reflecting mind. On the present occasion the principal use that she was making of them was to plague and tease Horace Vanzandt, as she had previously plagued and teased many other of the leading beaux of the village. Horace, however, was most particularly attractive game. He was handsome, lively, spirited, hot-tempered, and forgiving, so that it was the easiest thing in the world both to put him into a passion and to get him out of it; and these two exercises considerably varied the dulness of the village life. For Greyford was a dull village, it is to be confessed. Nobody was very rich there, and nobody was very poor. The girls were all educated at the high school, and knew and read and had heard about all sorts of scenes that they could not afford to see, and splendid doings in the world that they never could take any part in, and read serial stories every week out of three or four newspapers, by means of which they lived among duchesses and countesses, and had all sorts of thrilling adventures in the spirit, while their bodies were tied down to the routine of a narrow, economical family life. The young men at Greyford, as a matter of course, were put to work early, and hadn't half the time to read and study and get themselves up in poetry and romances that the girls had, and consequently there was none of them that appeared to the girls the ideal hero; but still they were accepted as the best there was. There were approved ways and means of seeing each other. There was the singing-school once a week, where, by the by, Nettie had the richest voice and led the treble. There were apple-cuttings and croquet-parties; but, best and liveliest of all, there were the sleigh-rides which came in the winter, when the young fellows were to a good degree released from farm-work, and free to bask in the charms of female society.

It had been given out and agreed among the young fellows of the village, that, as soon as there was snow enough, there should be a grand sleigh-ride over to the hotel in North Denmark, where a dancing-room had been engaged, and provision made for a regular frolic.

The point in discussion in Nettie's mind as she stood nodding at her image in the glass was this: Would Horace Vanzandt come to invite her to this sleigh-ride? She knew, in her own guilty conscience, that she had sent him off horridly angry the Sunday evening before, and whether he had gotten over it or not was the point in discussion in her own mind; and, by way of estimating the balance of probabilities, she took a good look at herself. She rather thought he would come back, and at this moment she heard the click of the gate. In a moment she turned, and was seated in the demurest manner at her work-basket, making a little ruffled apron with pockets, in which she was so much absorbed that Horace was obliged to rap three or four times on the door till he could rouse the ear of the little inattentive bound-girl in the back-kitchen. There had been times when Miss Nettie under such circumstances would go and open the door herself, and say, " Oh! is it you? I thought,"— &c., &c., &c. But this morning she felt diplomatic; and, on the whole, she concluded that he must be made to come all the way. Horace, in fact, had come resolved to beg pardon for being insulted on Sunday evening. He had flown into a passion and made himself ridiculous. Of course this had put him in the wrong; but now here was the snow coming, and he wanted Nettie for his partner. He knew that she would tease and provoke him the whole evening. Why, then, would no one else but Nettie do for him, when there was Jane Burgess, the nicest, sweetest, most reasonable girl that ever was heard of, who never did or said an unkind thing to anybody; and Rachel Holley, with cheeks and forehead like the pink and the white of sweet-peas and the prettiest and most winning of voices? Both these had graciously entreated him; and yet he could form no idea of anybody that he wanted except this vexatious Nettie, who neither would take him nor let him alone, and kept him always in a state of fermentation. Well, why does a young fellow like to drive a lively, high-spirited filly, that prances and curvets, snorts, and pulls on the bit, and comes within an inch of dashing his brains out every once in a while? We leave that to the consciousness of individuals and to the metaphysicians. All is, Horace has stood long enough on the door-step, and we must get him in.

CHAPTER II.

HORACE determined to open the matter cheerfully, and ignore the fact that there had been any quarrel; and so began briskly, "Well, Miss Sylva, we are in luck; the snow has come."

"I don't like snow," said Nettie, contradictiously; but she smiled as she said it, and, lifting her great, beautiful eyes, fixed them on Horace not unkindly.

"But don't you see, Miss Nettie, our sleigh-ride is to come off now?"

"Sleigh-ride?" said Miss Nettie, in a tone of innocent inquiry. "What sleigh-ride?"

"Why, of course you know: the sleigh-ride that we fellows have been planning for three or four weeks past. We've got the room and the fiddler all engaged."

Now, Nettie knew all these things perfectly well. The fact was, that she and Jane Burgess and Rachel Holley had discussed them over and over, to the minutest details of possibilities, and they had all settled what they were to wear. But

was she to let the enemy know this? Of course
not.

"Oh!" she said, "I can't be expected to know,
as nothing has been said to me."

"Why, of course," said Horace.

"I don't think it is of course," said Nettie.
"How should I know any thing, when nothing
has been said to me?"

"Why, yes; it is all arranged. Jeff Fleming is
to take Jane Burgess in his new sleigh. He went
to New Haven last week, and bought a new string
of bells on purpose; and Mark Hinsdale is going
with Rachel Holley; and may I have the pleasure,
Miss Nettie, of taking you?"

"Oh! it appears I am Hobson's choice, then.
Thank you. I don't know that I shall care to go.
It will be very cold, and I think sleigh-rides are
rather a bore."

"Now, Miss Sylva, you really can't be so
cruel."

"Cruel! I don't know what you call cruel.
Ah! I see what you mean. I suppose you have
tried all the other girls and found them engaged."

"I do think you are the most provoking person,
Miss Nettie, that ever I did know."

Horace Vanzandt was a very handsome young
fellow; and when he was angry the blood flushed
into his cheek, and the fire snapped from his eyes;

1*

and Nettie felt a perilous sort of pleasure in provoking these natural phenomena.

"Come now, Horace," she said suddenly, assuming an air of the most sisterly concern. "Why must we always quarrel? not that I care particularly about it, but it really grieves me to see a person that I respect give way to his temper so."

"By George! Nettie, it's your fault," said Horace. "I never do get so angry with anybody else, but you seem to delight to make me miserable. 'Now, I came to invite you on Sunday night, but you quarrelled with me and got it all out of my head." .

"Well, Horace, if you have come just to renew the Sunday night's quarrel" —

"I haven't. I came to make up."

"And give me Hobson's choice in the sleigh-ride," said Nettie.

Horace rose up hastily, and flung out of the room. Nettie gave one quick mischievous glance after him, seized a little packet from her work-basket, ran round by another path to the gate, and was there before Horace got there. "You silly boy," she said. "You never will give me time to give you this. I had it all ready for you on Sunday night."

It was a guard-chain of Nettie's own workmanship which had been promised to Horace months before.

"I 've sat up many a night working on this," she said reproachfully.

"O Nettie!"

"Come now, let's be friends," she said, laying her hand on his arm. "Really, Horace, I feel absolutely concerned about your violent temper. You must overcome it." Horace looked at her quizzically as she put the guard-chain round his neck, and then followed her an unresisting captive into the house again, where it pleased Nettie to keep him at her feet reading Tennyson to her till near dinner-time. And this was the way that matters commonly went on between Horace and Nettie.

Horace Vanzandt was the son of one of the largest farmers in the neighborhood, and the youngest of four brothers who all took respectably to farming. Horace was of a lively turn of mind, and meant to strike out something rather more adventurous and congenial in life. If there was any thing he detested it was following the slow steps of oxen, ploughing, and planting potatoes and harvesting little gains at the end of the year. Horace determined to be an inventor. He had a turn for machinery and a Yankee quickness of hand. He even in boyhood had made a pattern of a water-wheel which turned an imaginary mill in the brook in the back lot. He had devised a

churn for his mother, which the knowing ones
said might have taken a patent if somebody else
hadn't made one just like it before him. So Horace read and thought, and whittled, and studied
models, and used to carry them up to show to
Nettie, who sometimes laughed at them, but, after
all, rather fed the flame of his hopes and anticipa-
tions.

Nettie sympathized with all her fiery, restless
heart in Horace's contempt of farming, and in his
desires to make to himself a fortune in some easier
way. She detested the dull reality of life in Greyford, where, as she phrased it, "nobody ever came,
and nothing ever happened."

Greyford, to be sure, was one of those still,
quiet towns which impress travellers who ride
through it with the idea that the inhabitants are
all either dead or gone on long voyages. The
front doors were always tight shut even in the
warmest summer weather, and not a human creature was by any accident ever seen about them.
All the window-blinds were tight closed, except
perhaps one-half of one on one side, far to the
back of the house. The reason of this was, that
when the Greyford housekeepers had cleaned the
paint of the chambers and parlors, in the spring,
they wanted to keep them immaculate from flies,
and so shut up all the window-blinds till the time

for the autumn cleaning. Meanwhile they lived in one or two rooms in the back of the house, and congratulated themselves that the front part was always in order. This particular habit, by the way, though a most efficient preservative of the colors of carpets and conducive to the health and long life of the hair-seat chairs and chintz-covered sofas which lurked within these dark domains, was not acceptable to Master Horace. He used to say that when he had a house of his own he was going to set apart one room in it for a fly-room, and have it warm and bright and airy and sunny, and have just as many flies in it as he wanted. Nettie, when he said this one day in her presence, answered promptly, that if he went on in that contrary spirit he would find not only flies entering into his room, but Beelzebub the god of flies; whereupon Horace rejoined impulsively that he hoped to coax a goddess in there, not a devil. Then he stopped short, a little embarrassed. Nettie, however, with that instinctive readiness of which the shyest and most skittish young ladies have the most, answered with a sniff that he wasn't likely to catch many goddesses unless he baited his trap with something better than flies.

But, as we have said a few words about Greyford, we will make bold to say a few more; for the fact is, that this ancient town is itself better worth knowing, not merely than the two inexperienced young persons about whom we have been talking, but even than the whole of any one of the generations of hard-working, economical, humdrum New-Englanders, who have slowly followed each other to the old-fashioned dreary burying-ground of the town since its first settlement in the year 1639.

Greyford is one of the very oldest of the Connecticut towns, and, like all those which were portions of the original New Haven Colony, was settled in good measure by "gentry," as distinguished from the yeomanry, from whom almost exclusively the Connecticut colony was recruited. Hence its families have yet traditions and heirlooms that knit together with a strong but invisible tie the working-day life that now is, and the faraway days of the knights and gentlemen of Good Queen Bess and her successor Gentle King Jamie. These, however, are but few, — an ancient copy of the Geneva Bible, or a faded and almost invisible embroidered coat-of-arms. But of both the early and the later days of our history, the memorials were more numerous, and the recollections were clear and authentic, and romantic too. The sons of old Greyford, farmers though they were, bravely upheld the cause, and followed the banner of their country, whether it was the blood-red flag of the English king, or the brighter stars and stripes, from the old French War down to the Rebellion; serving always under officers of their own choice, wise and experienced fellow-townsmen of their own. Others had followed the sea, and had brought home with them to ornament the brown old homesteads where they established themselves to end their days, such strange and fantastic articles as sailors delight to gather.

Now the antique queen's arms and the old carved powder-horns, the whales' teeth and the New-Zealand clubs, startle and interest the visitor who finds them in a country farm-house, and set him thinking and questioning. In like manner these manifold experiences of war and seafaring had stored the minds of the dwellers in Greyford with many curious tales, and with travellers' thoughts and opinions, such as seem strange and uncanny to the dwellers-at-home, but yet are full of stimulus and fascination.

In such communities there are always such persons as we commonly term "characters." A retired sea-captain is certain to be a character. Long-forgotten strains of ancestral blood reappear all of a sudden in some curious manifestation in a plain farmer's son or daughter; and the child grows up perhaps into a genius, but oftener into a specimen of peculiarities — a character. And even

the life of the farmers who live and die at home,
utterly uneventful as it is, is in itself far from un-
favorable to the development of strange and odd
traits.   There is something in the calmness of the
sunny fields, in the stillness of winter snows, in
the cool quiet of the green woods, that conjures
certain minds into even an unnatural excitement,
even by the mystical influence of mere silent solitude.

The landscape of Greyford, and the character
of its surroundings, were so varied and picturesque
as to add great power to these natural influences.
There were broad tracts of ancient woodland,
stretching far away over the hills.   There was a
river, a clear and lively stream, that ran through
the township and entered the sea not very far
away.   There were broad and level tracts of
singularly fertile farming land.   Here and there
among the wooded hills of the back country were
lovely little lakes, all alone in the forest, and
plentifully stocked with perch and roach and pick-
erel, and well-known to many a barefooted boy as
the Meccas of his rare half-holidays.   At the extreme north-eastern part of the town, one steep
mountain, so isolated and so bold in its outline as
to seem much loftier than it really was, stood up
alone and silent, shrouded to its very summit in
thick, tall forest-trees, while the vast, sheer de-

scent of its eastern face plunged down in one immense cliff, far below the surface of the earth; for close under it was the largest of all the lakes of the whole region, whose steep shore, the continuation of the mountain precipice, sank into black waters reputed to be unfathomable. The road that led northward through this wild and striking pass had been scored deep into the living rock, for there was not a foot of level land to hold it.

Doubtless all these influences had moulded and modified more or less the traits of every personage in this our story; to which, having said all that we wanted to about geography and history, we now return.

Nettie had a painstaking step-mother, a worthy woman, devoted to the task of keeping her father's house in the required style. The relations between her and Nettie were diplomatic. Nettie was not fond of housework, and Mrs. Dr. Sylva was; and it occurred to the young lady, that, in this conjunction of circumstances, it was only the fair thing that her mother-in-law, who had the work to do, should arrange the house in her own way; though as we have intimated, it was a way extremely distasteful to Nettie. Still, rather than take hold with her own hands and conduct the housekeeping on another pattern, Nettie was will-

ing to let things take their course without remon-
strance. She had her own dresses to make and
alter according to the patterns in " Harper's Bazar,"
she had several serial stories on hand to read, and
she had the afore-named singing-schools, apple-
cuttings, croquet-parties, tea-drinkings, and sleigh-
rides to attend, and generally a love-affair off or
on; for Nettie was one of the sort who scarcely
ever made a visit without webbing some silly fly
in her net, and having a love-letter of some kind
to answer.

This conduct of Nettie's was very seriously dis-
approved, not only by the matrons of Greyford,
but by the young ladies of her set, who were
understood in confidential moments to aver to
each other that Nettie Sylva was a flirt, and that
it really was abominable for her to trifle with
gentlemen as she did.

But so long as Nettie found that the gentlemen
rather liked to be trifled with, and that their
hearts, however sorely scratched and lacerated by
her claws, had a marvellous aptitude for healing,
her own conscience was quite at ease in the matter. In fact, Nettie looked upon flirtation as the
only providential compensation her case admitted
of in her compulsory dull existence in Greyford.

Horace Vanzandt was, on the whole, rather
more to her than any of her other beaux; but then

Horace had no money, and there seemed no likelihood of his having any for years to come; so, as Nettie sensibly remarked, there was no sort of use in having any thing more than a friendship. But of course the gossips mated them, and they generally in point of fact were mated, as in the present sleigh-ride. Jeff Fleming never thought of such a thing as presuming to ask Nettie when Horace was evidently setting his cap in that direction; and Mark Hinsdale, though he had written a sonnet on her in "The Greyford Union Eagle," did not so much as venture to think of driving her in his sleigh on this occasion.

Nettie winced a little at times under this state of things. She wanted variety. "Who wants to be tied always to one fellow?" she remarked. Jane Burgess, on the contrary, had been heard to assert, that, if she had a friend as devoted to her as Horace was to Nettie, she would take more care how she treated him.

Jane was, to say the truth, just one of those women whom good mothers and sisters always wish their sons and brothers would marry. She was pretty, she was witty, and she was wise; but all in such just proportions, that there was no salient point. She was a girl of scruples, careful what she said and did, true to the heart's core, and without shadow of turning.

Nettie Sylva was a bundle of capabilities and perhapses. What she might become was a problem. She lived a life of impulse rather than reflection, and did things from morning till night for no other reason than that she felt like them at the moment. She belonged to the class celebrated by our respected friend Mr. Alexander Pope, —

> "Ladies, like variegated tulips, show
> 'Tis to their changes half their charms they owe."

Nettie certainly had as many streaks as a first-class tulip, and changes enough to make her extremely charming; and after Horace went away, she proceeded, with the aid of "Harper's Bazar," to compose a toilette for the next week's *fête* of the most killing description.

CHAPTER III.

HENRIETTA SYLVA put on her hat one afternoon, and went over to old Miss Burgess's. By "old Miss Burgess," I don't mean Jane. I never could bear to have people under any sort of misapprehension for a moment, even for the sake of an after agreeable surprise.

Old Miss Burgess is the aunt. Jane is the niece. Though, from living so long and so quietly with so prim and quaint a piece of the last generation, Jane had perhaps caught a flavor of the last generation herself, and mixed it up with her nineteen years in a certain gentle and odd suggestion of old-maidishness, that joins itself to her bloom and prettiness like a bit of thyme or lavender set in a bouquet; and she took on something auntlike in her ways among the girls. That is why Nettie Sylva, I think, liked her, and came to her, with all her little snarls that she could not pick out herself. Not for the help alone, either; she liked to shock the proper Jane, mildly, with her freaks and flights. For Jane took every thing in a calm, saint-like fashion, — even her shocks.

Jane Burgess was a pretty girl of the years-gone-by sort; one that could wear her hair plain and smooth to her head, twisted up behind, and have a dark calico gown on, without making any difference. The prettiness was there, — a fact; in the clear, pure, healthily-tinted skin; the open, fair contour; the large, deep, soft blue-gray eyes, with black, easily-dropping lashes; the even brows, the demure little nose, with perfect profile, the same both ways; and the delicious mouth, playing with a peculiar, tender, fascinating little curve of its own over the faultless, shyly visible teeth.

Once in a while of a warm summer's day, busy in her garden, or coming home from a walk; or in a crisp winter wind; or over the fire or the ironing board, in the flush of her work, — Jane's smooth brown hair would ruffle and wave itself into a soft mistiness and lightness about her forehead, and perhaps get pushed back in her forgetfulness from off her delicate temples; and then you saw one of those accidents of loveliness that never happen in these deliberately got-up days. Once, girls were liable to bewitching little unconscious changes; Nature had her own cunning tricks and manners with them; excitement or exercise lit them up, tossed them into pretty bewilderments of arrangement and color, and gave the looker-on little blessed revelations and sur-

prises: but now there must be bewilderment all
the time; they must turn away from their looking-
glasses all fluffed up with a cloudy confusion of
carefully dishevelled charms, that will not let any
line be traced throughout, but leaves artfully so
much to the imagination, — makes so many breaks,
like the shimmer of a veil, — that a general jumble
and sparkle imposes itself almost as a universal
beauty.   There is a certain amount of beauty
about; but you do not know exactly where it is,
any more than you do where the specie is that the
currency stands for.   Everybody gets temporarily
credited for a little.   It is pretty much so with all
our living, — even our thinking.   Life is broken
up into delusive rainbows.   There is hardly any
steady, pure, white light anywhere.

Old Miss Burgess met Nettie Sylva at the door,
her glasses pushed up against her cap, and her
long gray knitting-work in her hands.

"Jane has gone abroad this afternoon," she
said.   "But walk in; lay off your things, and stay
and drink tea.   She'll be proper glad to see you
when she comes.   You're quite a stranger."

Nettie Sylva knew what the old lady meant.
Jane had not gone to Europe.   We have not quite
arrived at the time, though it looks as if we might
be near it, when one can leave word with the
family, or with the serving-maid, as one puts one's

gloves on, — "I am going over in this afternoon's catapult; shall be back to tea," — take a shoot through the Liverpool tunnel and a half-hourly balloon to London, — make a few friendly calls, and hurry back at dusk.

No. Miss Burgess only meant, — in the old-fashioned way, used when nobody went more than a mile or two from home, except with grave preparation of scrip and staff, and making one's will beforehand, for weighty cause of life or love or property, — that Jane had gone for a walk in the village.

"I most wonder you didn't come across her somewheres," said the old lady, drawing her glasses down again, and poring over a dropped stitch. "She must be in to Squire Holley's."

When one of these three girls — Jane Burgess, Nettie Sylva, or Rachel Holley — missed another, she was pretty sure to turn up in company with the third. They were as different as the three angles of a scalene triangle, and just as essential to each other in the making up; especially at a time like this, when a grand frolic was afoot, invitations given and pending, and gowns to be decided on; to say nothing of feminine tactics and councils of war for the campaign.

Nettie Sylva came to Jane Burgess for nice little moral lectures and wise counsel; but then in a sly, keen fashion, she often turned round upon her before they finished their talk, and gave quite as good as she got.

"Now, what on earth am I to do with that Horace?" she says to Jane, leaning over the bureau while that particular young lady folded up and put away her shawl and gloves; Nettie, meantime, taking sidelong peeps at the looking-glass, trying to examine her own profile, which she was never quite satisfied with when she saw Jane's.

"It's the fox and the goose and the basket of corn. If I say no, and stay at home, there's my own poor little nose cut off, you see, — if it's pretty to say so; if I go with anybody else, — oh, my gracious! wouldn't there be a ferment and a rumpus? And if I undertake to go all that six miles with him alone, I shall either have to jump out into a snowbank and run home, or keep up such a squabble as I really haven't conscience or constitution for, or else hear all he's got to say; and I ain't ready, Jane Burgess! I've quarrelled with him till I'm tired."

"What do you quarrel with him for?"

"What else can I do? It isn't safe to stay made up with him half an hour. It's the only way a girl has to get time for herself. There's no fairness in it. A man can stand off, and look, and

2

consider, till he's made up his mind; and then he can come forward, and 'be particular;' and you can't let him begin to be the least bit particular without giving him claims; and how on earth you're to be fair to yourself and decent with him, I can't make out!"

"I suppose the girl has the same time to look and consider that the man has," said quiet Jane.

"Yes, indeed! And then what if he never begins? I tell you it's all on one side, and I believe I won't have any thing to do with it!"

And Nettie pouted, and felt the tears coming into her eyes, and saw the pins on Jane's cushion begin to glitter and grow big; and then she glanced round into the glass again, to find out how she looked when she was crying.

"I think it is ordered, if we only try to do what is right," said Jane, virtuously.

"Yes; and how are you going to know? If you look at a thing all round, there are so many rights. It's right for me to work myself out, and find out what I am, and what I want, and let him see. I've no business to be all Sylva and no Nettie, till after I'm married, and then drop it, as I've got to do. And he ought to be willing; it's for his good: he ought to take time for his own sake; but men never do. They are always in a hurry."

It is funny to see how a girl who comes to have affairs to manage with one man, talks immediately of the whole sex in a generalizing way, and feels as if she had all mankind at once upon her hands, and *vice versa.*

Well, it is true in a sense. They do stand to each other, representatively and inclusively, as man and woman; it is always, in each new experiment, Adam and Eve again, whatever else they may happen to have been christened.

"There is one thing that is always right," said Jane. "Not to do any thing, ever so little, to draw a man on, unless you are sure you are "— She paused shyly, with a bit of a blush rising.

"Smashed yourself!" said Nettie, boldly. "And how are you going to know when you *are* smashed? Or how are you ever likely to be till you have knocked round a little? That's the point. You can't buy a pair of shoes without trying 'em on. It's ridiculous!"

She began again presently.

"Mrs. Sylva says it's very 'shallow' of me not to know my own mind. That's a great word of my stepmother's. But if I were shallow, really, I don't think I should have any trouble. I tell you it's just sounding, and doubting, and considering that makes me act so. There are so many sides to every thing; and somehow I always see the

opposite one. That's the reason I quarrel; and
then, again, that's the reason I make up."

"If I imagined I ever might marry a person,"
said Jane thoughtfully, "I shouldn't want to have
all these little fusses beforehand. I shouldn't
think he would depend so much on me afterwards."

"I don't want to be depended on. I want him
to be thankful every day for what he gets, as we
all are; not knowing how long it's going to last.
That's Christian."

"Christian for him," said Jane quietly.

"And if I sanctify him, what better can I do?
That brings up the 'ordering' again. Do you
believe people are cut out for each other, Jane?
I don't. If they are, I should like to know who
does it."

"I think the Lord does," said Jane. "At any
rate, he brings people together."

"It's fixed very queer," said Nettie meditatively,
with a puzzled frown knit up into her forehead.
"Because you can't allow for the growing. It has
to be all settled before you really come to any
thing. As if things had been fitted on to me when
I was five years old to last all my lifetime. That's
no way for — anybody — to cut out! And I don't
believe anybody can. How do I know what I
shall be ten years from now? Or Horace Van-

zandt, either? It is an *awful* long measuring!
Now I think of it, that was the way mother used
to do with my gowns when she first came. She
made them down to my heels, for fear I should
outgrow them. And I hated them: they were
never right. I won't begin life so, all of a draggle,
because I shall be up higher by and by; neither
do I want to be left anyways unprovided for or
out in the cold, when I do get bigger. It isn't
fair! We ought to be made so as to keep *pretty*
longer, and have some chances!" And Nettie
ended, as usual, with a look in the glass.

"The best way is to make things that can be
let out and let down for the growing," Jane said.
"There is more in everybody than they know of,
I suppose. And the Lord, making the measures,
knows it all, doesn't he?"

"I presume it's proper to say he does," said
Nettie. "Jane! what are you going to wear
Thursday?"

"My stone-colored brilliantine, with blue rib-
bons, and some white chrysanthemums in my
hair."

"There, now! That's just you! All so easy
and quiet, and ready beforehand, and no-kind-of-
consequence-what; and, after all, you'll be the
very prettiest one. Rachel is going to be wonderful, though. Did she tell you! That new

dazzle-blue merino, with swan's-down round the neck and sleeves."

" I saw it.   What is yours ? "

" Crimson, with a flash in it.   Tea-rosebuds and coral flowers.   My roses are just blooming on purpose.   I shall carry them in a box on wet cotton-wool.   Won't Horace get into a fry while he's waiting down stairs for me to put them on?   And then, while he's getting over it, I'll be promising for half the dances to everybody that asks.   He always loses the next thing while he's rebelling about the last.   He's got lots to learn. . Jane! I'll just tell you what, — I've as good a mind as ever was to take Jeff Fleming in the pairing-off."

Jane colored up suddenly; then as suddenly calmed down and smiled.

" You think he *won't?* We'll see. Jane, you're altogether *too* settled. You're just as bad, the other way, as I am. And there's one thing, — I dare say you've no idea of it, — but I doubt if any thing makes much difference to you, after all. It happens to be Jeff, because you've had him at your elbow all your days, and it's ' cut out.' The truth is, *you* a'n't cut out for anybody in particular so much as just for a pattern. You'll be sweet and mild, and you'll be married, and you'll housekeep, just because it's all a part of perfect living for a woman; and *that's* what you're in love with. Jeff will do as well to hang it on to as anybody; and you'll live and die in a frame of mind like a pan of milk. And you'll set, and you'll just turn to solid, tranquil bonny-clabber. Now, *I*'m going to be either butter or cheese; I haven't made my mind up which. I've got 'em both in me. Isn't that queer?"

And she followed Jane downstairs into the corner sitting-room, where Miss Burgess was cutting up spice-cake for tea; and of course there was not much more said except about how her mother did, and whether the doctor thought old Deacon Chowle was any better, and how Jane had found Mrs. Holley this afternoon; Mrs. Holley being an invalid, and so always a staple of conversation. And at six o'clock, the starlight already shining over the snow, Nettie set off for home, meeting Jeff Fleming at the gate as she went out, and encountering Horace Vanzandt afterwards at the post-office, as she had every reason to expect she might, and letting him walk home with her for such consolation as he could get by the way, with all her little defensive prickles set up and alert whichever way he tried to stroke her.

If Horace Vanzandt had not been of the inventive order of mind, fond of puzzles, and given to combating little wearying obstacles with a most fine and patient and delicate ingenuity, the mere

man that was in him must have revolted long ago
at Nettie's whims, and thrown the whole thing
over.   But I thing the mechanician could not give
up the fascinating perplexity.   The more he was
baffled, the more the wheels would not run and
the cogs would not catch, the more he was irresist-
bly drawn to pursue the reason why, — the more
nicely and curiously he tried time after time to
adapt his experiments.   If he flung every thing by
in a pet, it was only to make himself more work in
repairing intricate and involved damages, when he
came back, penitent and patient, as in the nature
of him he could not help doing, to his task again.

CHAPTER IV.

RACHEL HOLLEY sat reading to her mother in the little bedroom that opened from the long sitting-room, until five o'clock; then Roxana came in with Mrs. Holley's tea, and Rachel kissed her mother, and went off to her own room to dress. For this was Thursday evening; and Mark Hinsdale was to come for her at half-past six, to drive her to North Denmark for the sleigh-ride dance.

Rachel Holley's toilet was even a prettier thing than the result; but we have no right to look at it, — to see the fresh pink of her face, and the white of her arms and shoulders as they come clear and blooming from under the dashes of cold water and the soft wrapping and pattings of the towel; to watch her brush her little set of pearls, and hear the pure, *whole* sound that tells of their perfection and entireness; but when the little pink sack is on, and that sunshine of hair is tossed down over it, like the golden over the rose in a fair sunset, — then, if I am ever to take author's privilege, and give you a peep at any picture you could

2*   c

not have without me, it becomes my duty to let you in.

Rachel's hair "did itself." It rippled and poured over her shoulders like an amber waterfall, with all the million little braided lines in it that curl and twist in running water; and the comb stroked through, just proving that it was not a tangle, but leaving every little curl and twist to reassert itself in its wake, precisely as the running water would if you drew your fingers through it. And then Rachel gathered it all up in her two little hands, that had to clutch and grasp to do it, and gave it a turn one way, and set in a little trident of shell to hold it, and after that a turn another way, burying the tiny comb, and now a long, slender hairpin was pushed in; and so round and round, here and there, caught and looped and fastened just as it seemed to be determined to go, until it was one beautiful, bewildering, shining heap, lying gracefully around the natural curves of her head, and dropping with a lovely, glistening shimmer about her brows and temples. You can't do it with tails and cushions and hot slate-pencils, and you needn't try; Rachel Holley just *had* that hair, and it was a piece of her. Jane Burgess's was pretty in its soft, modest, shadowy smoothness. Why don't you all keep what is your own? Then everybody would have something.

A blue ribbon was drawn through to finish, and tied in a little butterfly bow up high among the gold, on the left side ; and then, after the dainty fingers had been into the basin again, the dazzle-blue merino went on, and the snowy down border-ings were fastened about throat and arms, and — there was Rachel Holley ready for the sleigh-ride. And what do you think will become of Mark Hins-dale now ?

Poor little Rachel ! I had to bring you up here to see her, without telling you why. You must needs have had this one unspoiled glimpse of her glad beauty. Even Mark Hinsdale was not to see it after all, — *just so,* — to-night.

She turned round with her candle in her hand, to go downstairs. A rapid step came up as she opened her door. Roxana's frightened face met hers.

"O Rachel, for the land's sake hurry down! Your ma ! "

Mrs. Holley was " taken faint," as Roxana called it. They gave her brandy, and sent the boy, Silas, for the doctor. Rachel rubbed her mother's hands, and sent Roxy for the hot brick from the oven, to put to her cold feet. She bathed her head with bay-water, and gave her carefully some drops of hartshorn to smell at. And then, while she came slowly back to some-

thing like her usual frail, delicate life again, yet
with a new, strange look that shot a fearful intui-
tion straight to Rachel's heart, and made it seem
an unreckoned duration of experience since she
had tied on her blue ribbon so unconsciously there
upstairs, — a look as of one who leaves the door,
but turns back for a thing yet to be fetched or
done, — Rachel sat, and knelt, and stood, by or
over her, tending, and listening, and whispering,
and making little loving signs, for half an hour,
alone with her, while they waited. For Mrs. Holley had feebly motioned to Roxana to go away.

I cannot tell you. of that half-hour. It was a
half-hour between two dear souls; a little time
God gave them to live in, — to go back into from
either side and meet in, as the heart and secret
and fulness of their years together, by and by,
when they should be outwardly parted.

There are points of experience where all things
gather. Eternity is in them. They are like the
three short years of the Lord Christ's ministering
to the world.

When Mark Hinsdale came, Mrs. Holley had
fallen into a brief sleep.

Mark thought it was some beautiful, tender-sad
angel who came so softly through the shadow of
the sitting-room to meet him, and stood in the
firelight in her azure robes with shining borders.

For there was something glorified, uplifted above the shock and the fear, in Rachel's face, strong and full of love from that supreme communion.

"Mother is going to die," she said, putting her hand in Mark's, and raising that look, that he never forgot, to his.

"Oh, no!" he said with the first pitying impulse, keeping hold of the hand. "Is she worse? She will be better again, as she has been. Don't be frightened."

"I'm not frightened. I *see*. O Mark!" she said suddenly, as one tender heartbreak from their deep, brief talk came over her, — "she said — she — shook me once — when I was a little child, — and she asked me to forgive her!"

And the human grief broke forth in passionate tears. Mark put his arm around her, as she stood and trembled with her sobs.

"Don't cry! don't cry, Rachel!" was all he could say to her.

And Dr. Sylva came in and found them so.

Squire Holley was away from home, attending to some law business. Instead of going to North Denmark, Mark Hinsdale drove his fast bay colt all night over the road to Hartford, and brought the squire back next morning in time to see his wife.

The next time Mark saw Rachel, it was in a black dress at her mother's burial.

Dr. Sylva was a sympathetic man, and a bit of a friendly old gossip. He was touched and interested by what he had seen, and he could not help talking about it. He told how good Mark Hinsdale had been, and how plain it was that all was settled between him and Rachel. "And the sooner it's made fast the better," he said. "Squire Holley's rich enough to take them both right in at home. And I guess that's the way it will be. He won't want to part with his girl; and yet he's no kind of a man to be left in charge of her, all alone, though he's first-rate for the deestrict."

And that was the way that everybody came to have it that Mark Hinsdale and Rachel Holley were engaged.

CHAPTER V.

NOBODY knew at the sleigh-ride dance what was happening. They all wondered and wondered, between the cotillons, and in hands across, and up and down the reels, what had be-come of Mark and Rachel. Some thought one thing, and some another, according to their own characteristics. Jeff Fleming said Mark was in one of his clouds somewhere, and had forgotten to come down. Nettie Sylva guessed they had had some little muss: they would come in late, maybe, with some excuse, just in time, perhaps, for the pairing-off. Jane quietly remembered Mrs. Holley, and thought she might have needed Rachel; but nobody imagined any thing like the truth. There is no one whom all the world looks upon as more a fixture *in* the world, than a confirmed invalid.

Nettie Sylva had tied her face up in a cloud, and told Horace he must not talk to her, coming over; she had had a toothache yesterday, and was afraid of it again. What with that, and dropping her muff out of the sleigh and making him go back for it through the snowdrifts, and taking it into her head to carry the whip and touching up the gay little mare with it almost every time Horace did say any thing, she got over the ground, according to her notion of it, pretty well.   The rest of the programme had been carried out very nearly as she had indicated it to Jane.   She had been a long time settling the exact position of the tea-roses in her bright, silky crimps, and in making them " stay put ; "   for tea-rosebuds, everybody knows, are the loveliest and most unmanageable of blossoming things, — they are so tipsy with their own rich beauty ; and, by the time she came down from the little gallery dressing-room attached to the dancing-hall, she found Horace in the passage below, tolerably cold, and in a fair state of provokableness.   Everybody else, nearly, had gone in.

" Have you been ready long ? " she asked sweetly, taking his arm.   " But then you didn't have tea-rosebuds to fix in your hair !   Let's make haste now : they 'll be engaging for all the dances, and I don't want to be left out in the cold."

That last clause was a sudden impish inspiration.

" I suppose not.   Nobody does," said Horace,

with an enunciation as if his words were just
stiffening with frost as he spoke them, and were
too much congealed to flow further after those
five.

" Why, you 're all nipped up ! " said Nettie,
turning round at him. " Your nose is blue.
You 'd better go right to the fire, and get warm.'

And with that, she dropped his arm as they got
inside the door, and let herself be surrounded, at
the instant of his half withdrawal, by two or three
eager claimants for dancing promises.

The second dance, and the third, and the fourth,
she gave. Nobody asked for the first, of course ;
that was supposed, according to sleigh-ride etiquette, to be Horace's.

When she had reached as far as five, she looked
round to see where Horace was. He was standing by the big wood fire, half-way down the hall ;
warming his nose, probably, as she had bidden
him.

" Good boy ! " she said slyly to herself, under
her breath, and laughed.

Then she slipped off, quite at the opposite side,
and along to a far corner, where she seated herself demurely.

The first set was forming. Clarissa Dunmore
was standing up there in the corner, with her
brother Elisha. Nettie got behind Miss Dun-

more's wide skirts, — for Clarissa only had a new
best dress once in three years, and wore the fashion
out, — and hid herself. She chattered with Miss
Clarissa as she came back and forth, and made
her miss half the figures.

" Why ain't you dancing ? " was Miss Clarissa's
natural question.

" Oh, I 'm getting ready ! Hands across ! Why
don't you mind ?   There 's Nat Kinsley, waiting ! "

Nettie knew she could always manage Miss
Clarissa.

Clarissa was an old maid and didn't know it.
She had never stopped to think about it.   She had
only had four best dresses since she began to keep
house for her brother after their mother died ; and
she had gone about with him to all the sleigh-rides
and huskings and apple-bees, ever since, quite
naturally ; for neither of them had anybody else
to go with.   Clarissa thought her time hadn't
come, if she thought any thing, and kept on
patiently ; not expecting to be " run after much,"
because she had never been a beauty ; but just
accepting things as they were, and putting a piece
of daphne odora, off her big bush, into her back
hair, just where she had put it twelve years ago,
and setting off contentedly with Elisha every time
there was a merry-making, and seeing it all

through, with him to depend upon, and to talk it over with afterward.

" Elisha was real clever and good about seein' to," she said : " she didn't know what girls did that didn't have brothers."

They danced as much as they wanted to ; for " they always had one another, if nobody else came along." And they really supposed they had " been to the party," as much as anybody else. Some people take the world at large in that way, and think they have been to it too.

After the cotillon was over, Nettie scudded round again, and got on to the opposite side, met the girls, Jane Burgess and three or four others whom she knew best, who all supposed, of course, that she had been dancing. Then she came up face to face with Horace Vanzandt, just as she meant to do.

" Oh ! " she cried. " Why where have you been ? I didn't see any thing of you all through the set. Have you got warm yet ? "

" I hope you had a pleasant dance," said Horace grimly.

" Dance ! why, I *didn't* dance. Of course not. I sat over there in the corner all the time. Nobody asked me. I haven't had a soul to' speak to but Clarissa Dunmore and Elisha. *I'm* getting cold now."

"Nettie!" said Horace, in a low, strong voice, "what does all this mean?"

"I don't — know — I'm *sure!*" said Nettie, with wide-open brown eyes. "What does it? I — supposed" —

"What?"

"Well, — if you *will* make me say it, — that you might possibly have asked me to dance, yourself; and so I waited."

There could not be any thing more utterly simple than Nettie's look lifted up to Horace Vanzandt's face.

"If that is all, come and dance now," said Horace, holding out his hand, with a very grave face. It was earnest with him: he could not stop for jests, scarcely for courtesies.

"Oh, *now* I'm engaged! For this, and the next, and the next, and the next. And, besides, I think it would be proper to say 'sorry' or 'please,' or something!"

And Nettie went off with Jeff Fleming. "Jeff was bright," she said: "she always had a good time with Jeff Fleming," she told Jane.

Horace Vanzandt went and asked Jane.

Somehow, when Nettie was very bad, he had an impulse toward Jane Burgess for friendly comfort. Jane knew Nettie so well, and always had something kind and excusing to say, that made him feel better.

"I can't make Nettie out to-night," he said, while he and Jane waited at the side.

"You never can," said Jane. "That's just what she means. If you didn't try you'd do better."

"But why does she treat me so? She went off and made me think she had been dancing, and then came back and put me in the wrong because I hadn't asked her. She makes me — mad; and then she won't give me any excuse for a quarrel; nothing to take hold of, I mean."

"Don't look for it. Take it as if it were all right. It is only a part of the frolic. Nettie is a good girl, only she isn't quite ready to sober down. You mustn't — hurry her."

Jane colored up as she said this. It was the nearest to a taking-for-granted of 'Horace's wish and meaning toward Nettie, that she had ever come to in any of their tacit confidences.

They had to chassé now, and Horace could not say any more until the figure was over. He thought what a nice quiet partner Jane was, as he came back to her, and met her clear, friendly look and pleasant smile. It rested him to be with her a while. She was like fair, level road, after ups and downs, jolts and pitches. But then that, he supposed, was because he didn't care so much. What was it that kept him beating back and forth helplessly, among the thorns and tangles of Nettie's tricks and whims?

"I wish she would grow more like you, Jane. Can't you make her? You are together so much."

"You wouldn't like her half so well," said Jane, smiling at his question. It did not seem so surprising a question to her, doubtless, as it would have done if she had not known in her quiet way that she *was* a pattern. To her mind there was only one sort of woman that was worth while, or that ever ought to be; and she meant to be that woman right straight through. Of course Nettie would be better if she could make her a little more after the same type; but then she spoke truth and wisdom in saying that Horace — at this stage of his experience, at least — would not have liked her half as well.

"See how pretty she is this minute! And sweet and happy too: there isn't a bit of real malice in it. It's all fun."

Nettie was flying out across the hall in a long gallopade chassé, her color bright, her dark eyes like two winter stars, and a merry gleam of glittering teeth between the red parted lips.

She came quite up to them as they stood.

"I shan't have a dance left," she said, in a gay, quick whisper to Jane, as she gave her a little whirl, and then took her partner's hand again.

" If anybody else wants one," she added, over her shoulder, " he 'd better make haste. But it 's a reel next ; and I *won't* engage for reels, ever ! "

" You heard ? " said Jane.

" Yes. She meant me to."

" Of course she did. That 's the good of her. She has kept the reel on purpose."

" She always keeps the reels. She likes to set them scrambling. And I won't scramble." For all that, he got beside her when the quadrille ended. Jane managed it partly, perhaps, in choosing her seat.

" Will you dance with me now ? " said Horace, when the reel was called. And Nettie gave him her hand with an exquisite little docile, nestling, good-child movement to his side. Nettie was lovely all through that reel, and the next, which came in two dances more. " I always like my best dances in the middle of the evening," she said. " The first ones are dreary." And Horace grew content under her smiles, as he had done a hundred times before, and let by-gones be by-gones, as Nettie always told him he ought ; although she did confess to Jane Burgess that the by-gones were never more than twenty-four hours old before they began again.

Jane herself could hardly tell what to make of Nettie, when she declared to her in the " join hands " of Money Musk, that she " didn't more than half like it, after all: she believed if he would only stay mad, once, long enough to give her a real little scare, she should like him better than she ever had done yet."

"But he knows you don't mean it. He could see you didn't, the minute he quieted down. Besides, I told him so."

"You did! You were nicely set to work! Now I shall have it all to do over again!"

She did it in the pairing-off.

The pairing-off was the last dance of all. Nettie had been down to supper, — and I wish I could tell you all about that supper, such as is only had in a country tavern, at a country sleigh-ride; its roast chickens and ducks, its whipped creams and plum-cakes, its custards and quince jellies, its nuts and apples, and cheese and crullers; its hot coffee, thick with cream, and its champagne cider; its regular sitting down, pair and pair; its plentiful helpings; its jokes and its fortune-tellings and its philopenas, with apple-parings and apple-namings, and double almonds. I should like to tell you all; but there will not be room for every thing, and I can't: I can only tell you, as I began to do, that Nettie behaved beautifully, — as beautifully as Nature and little children do before some grand outburst of mischief; and she came up again radiant and benign, and danced the "Rustic" with Horace, with Cla-

rissa Dunmore, whom she had made him take for
his other partner. And Horace said to himself how
good-natured and thoughtful that was of her for the
poor thing, after all.

But when the pairing-off came!

That is a round dance; not what we call a round
dance here in the city, but a dance formed in a ring.

No one takes a partner: they all go up one by one
and take places independently, — a young man and
a young woman alternately; though I will not say
there may not be some mutual management to get
tolerably near each other in certain cases. Yet
that is not sure to avail, either; for it rests with
the manager to call out as he pleases, " Ladies to
the right, gentlemen to the left! " or the reverse.
And then follows something like the old Swiss
dance, — a forward and back, a turning round, a
passing on; so that, one after another, each lady
meets every gentleman. And as they meet, — by
settled agreement, by some quick, mutual understanding, or by deliberate asking and assent, as the
case may be, — they pair off, here and there;
chassé together out from the ring and round the
circle, and to places, successively, in a long line
gradually formed from the top of the room, for
contra-dance; and then a merry hands-across, down
the middle and up again, down the outside and up
the middle, — a scamper to the end, — and all re-

peated, as long as any couple cares to keep it up, finishes, with its gay tumult, the evening.

Horace Vanzandt placed himself in the ring next but three to Nettie. Nat Kinsley, Elisha Dunmore, and Jo Greenleaf were between. She *wouldn't* take either of them, he thought.

But Jeff Fleming gave the word, " Ladies to the left ! " and behold the whole circle was between them ! He could only trust now to her love of fun and dancing, and the likelihood of her coquetting all round the set before she took up with any.

He watched at every turn ; she made seven or eight, and then she met Jeff Fleming. How she did it nobody knew, of the three most interested ; least of all, perhaps, Jeff himself, who certainly had thought of nothing until that moment but of looking out for Jane. But just as he gave his hands to Nettie, in the turn, he met a sudden, shy, merry, mischievous, wistful little glance — he was conscious of the least possible lingering as they came around, — of a little tremulous poise of her pretty figure ; their eyes encountered again, with a flash of fun in both ; and away out to the far side with a sweep, down again toward the lessening circle around, and up to the head of the hall triumphantly, the naughty couple ran away with each other before the assembled eyes of Greyford and North Denmark.

Horace made a few turns more, and then broke out of the ring and sat down. That, also, the dancers were at liberty to choose. That made the more fun. Two or three others got tired, or foresaw that it might be policy, and did the same ; Jane paired off with Elisha Dunmore ; and Clarissa, trotting round patiently to the end, expecting nothing but the dance, was left out, odd, at last ; and, nothing troubled, went quietly off to the dressing-room, to find her hood and rubbers comfortably before the crowd came up.

Down at the door, when all was over, Horace met Nettie Sylva, in her wraps, nothing visible in her face but two brilliant, provoking eyes.

" I'm *so* sorry, Horace ! but I don't dare ride in that cutter again. My toothache has come back ; and so I'm going with Mr. Dunmore in his chaise-top. You'll take Clarissa, *won't* you ? "

CHAPTER VI.

A LETTER.

New York, Dec. 1, 1870.

DEAR NETTIE, — I think I was right in leaving Greyford without giving you notice. The fact is, if I had told you, I am afraid I should not have come. You have great power over me; so much that I have run away from it. I cannot bring myself to submit any longer to be treated as you treat me, even by one whom I admire as much as you, and of whom I think as much as I do of you. And I found that I was man enough to quietly pack up and go; and so I did.

Now that I am here, and established, it is right again that I should tell you about it. And still I am conscious that you will perhaps be displeased, and will not care to know. However, I am assistant book-keeper at Fylings & Co.'s Works. They do many kinds of manufacturing in iron, and they rent parts of their building, together with the use of steam-power, to mechanics; so that the fact is, the place is a sort of paradise to me. If I should

ever go to heaven, I sometimes fancy I shall find
my part of it fitted up with all kinds of machinery
and tools, one eternal buzz of gearing and belts,
and lathes and planers, and all manner of artificers
in brass and iron. My patron saint is St. Tubal
Cain, I guess. I have already scraped acquaintance with a wiry little man, with great, thoughtful
eyes, who is working all day, and thinking all day
and all night too, upon a new type-setting and
distributing machine.

I have seen Rachel two or three times. Poor
girl! She was always so bright and happy that I
never imagined she had such depth and intensity
of feeling. And her mother had been ill so long,
and her hold on life was so very frail, that I should
have reasoned that her departure would have been
a comfort rather than a sorrow. But all the way
from Greyford she was so sad and silent that I
could not talk to her. And when last evening
I said something about her mother, she trembled
so much and cried so much that I was frightened.
I cried a little too. I don't know but I ought to
be ashamed of it, but I never yet saw tears of real
sorrow without contributing a few. I don't remember crying on my own account, either, since
I was small enough to cry at being whipped. I
don't know why it was, but I somehow felt that
in some way or other, something about Mark had

been the reason of Rachel's leaving Greyford. And yet I can't see why; for everybody was noticing how kind Mark was, and how suitable it would be if they should be married at once and go to the Squire's to live. But she would not say a word about Mark; and though I can't tell what made me know, I did know, that she did not wish to. I am sorry for Mr. Holley, left alone in the old house. But then he is one of those who find a great deal to satisfy their minds in their business; so he will do very well.

I have read this over. I have left out, I guess, the things I would have liked best to say. But, Nettie, I don't know how you would take them. And I am waiting to hear what you say to me. I suppose I have everybody's ordinary privilege to say that I am

Truly yours — haven't I?

HORACE VANZANDT.

THE ANSWER.

HARTFORD, Dec. 7, 1870.

DEAR HORACE, — Your letter was forwarded to me from Greyford, and so I could not answer any sooner.

It was extremely kind of you to reveal to me the place of your abode, in case I should be anxious to know. I should be very proud to believe that I had so much influence over you as you kindly intimate. But if your letter can be relied upon, you will not miss me very much as long as you can have a machine to turn round and round.

I was not so much surprised to hear of your going to New York as if you had never spoken of it to me. And I do not know why you should imagine that I would have remonstrated with you. You write as if I were a kind of evil genius whom you found it necessary to avoid. This I assure you is a mistake. I am truly your friend. But I hope I should not have distressed you by crying as Rachel did, if you had been brave enough to come and tell me what you were going to do.

As you have told me about your situation, I suppose I may tell you about mine. I am staying with my Aunt Helen, helping her keep house, and taking lessons in singing and the piano, besides hers in housekeeping. Aunt Helen wanted me to come, and Mrs. Sylva did not object, though father did.

It will always give me pleasure to hear from you. NETTIE.

P. S. Jeff Fleming is in Hartford now. He came with me. He is real good company. He is clerk in a store, and they say he has been making some first-rate speeches before the Sons of Tem-

perance. Nobody knew he was so smart — except
me. I always said he was bright. He is quite
attentive, which is very proper to his old friend,
all alone here in the busy city.

I am so glad you are comforting poor Rachel.
She is so good that I only wonder she should need
any comfort. When you see her give her my best
love.

You will, perhaps, be interested to hear that
Mark Hinsdale has gone to Boston to live, and
that Jane Burgess has gone there too. I don't
know exactly what they are doing; but no doubt
Rachel will hear from Mark, and tell you all about.
Jeff Fleming has not heard yet, except that Jane
is visiting her sister, Mrs. Bardles, and is having
a kind of holiday. It is as if a mine had exploded
under us six, and flung us helter-skelter, six ways
for Sundays. I suppose it will all be right, however; fates will be served out to us, I guess, at
the rate of about six to the half-dozen. That will
be just right: a fate apiece.   NETTIE.

Now, the intelligent reader will have observed
that these two letters were like the stories of for-
ests and enchantments drear, which Milton speaks
of, —

"Where more is meant than meets the ear."

They afforded no bad specimens, in fact, of

topics which shine by their absence. Horace did not tell Nettie that he was grieved by her conduct or sorry for his own. Nor did Nettie tell any thing of the kind to Horace. Like two Yankees, as they were, they were talking about the weather and the crops, instead of coming right down to their bargain.

Horace's letter did not surprise Nettie particularly, for he had often talked to her of his schemes of fortunes to be made in the city; but hers did somewhat startle him, and it annoyed him too. But it was his own fault; for he had written, in his displeasure, a stiffish and rather presuming letter, to tell the truth. What business had he to assume that it was such a mighty concern of hers whether he left Greyford or not? And then the innuendo, twice over, that she must profess a deep interest in his goings-on or else he wouldn't say a word about them! It was not a very judicious piece of diplomacy, truly.

If it had told the whole truth, however, instead of telling not half, but one-third of it, so to speak, it would have been still less judicious; that is, always supposing that Master Horace had intended to propitiate. But the young gentleman had thought fit to conceal from Nettie a still more striking expression of that emotional sympathy which he had described than that which he did mention.

3*

The fact is, that, quite carried away by poor
Rachel's tears, Horace had at parting quietly put
his arm round her and kissed her, — on the forehead, I mean, in a beautifully brotherly way; and
the poor girl, nervous and fluttered, did not think
of resisting.

In short, though Horace was not exactly conscious of it, his letter was cold and irritating, well
calculated to provoke Nettie, who, whatever she
might be in the depths of her nature, was a sufficiently high-spirited and independent puss, little
disposed to be ordered about by anybody. The
proof of this, indeed, had already come to pass
before Horace wrote, although he knew nothing of
it; and not mistrusting any such state of things,
this it was which startled him as aforesaid.

One fine day, then, a short time after the evening of the dance at North Denmark, Dr. Sylva
brought home the news of Horace's departure,
with a good deal of perturbation in his kindly old
heart as to its bearings upon his daughter's happiness. He gave it first to his wife, along with an
open letter, and he requested the good lady to
transfer the two to Nettie; for he had a vague idea
that where there's any thing uncomfortable, women
should be dealt with by women. N. B. It's a
great mistake!

Mrs. Sylva was a little hampered by considera-

tions like these about either happiness or circum-
spection; being one of those well-meaning and
thick-skinned persons who blurt right out whatever occurs to them to say, and look with the most
honest surprise at any one who talks about hurting
people's feelings. She marched straightway to the
foot of the stairs, and bawled out, —

"Nettie! Nettie! here's Horace Vanzandt he's
gone to New York 'long with Rachel Holley, n'
here's a letter for you f'm Hartford!"

Nettie, busy in her own room, felt her heart
give a jump, and then it sank with that painful
lost feeling that sudden bad news brings. But as
she was alone, nobody saw her; and she turned
first pale and then red; and the tears filled her
eyes, and she succeeded in preventing them from
running over; and it was with a delay scarcely
perceptible that she ran downstairs and received
the letter, answering her step-mother's communi-
cation very composedly with, —

"Well, Horace Vanzandt has been talking long
enough about going, and it's time he went, I'm
sure!"

She very soon read her aunt's letter, and very
promptly accepted its invitation, much against the
wishes of the worthy doctor. But Nettie argued
with much briskness and force that this was exactly the occasion she had been waiting for to take

some finishing lessons in singing and on the piano, and moreover in the ways of the "Old Hartford Housekeepers;" a generation of ancient dames who are traditionally reported to have possessed mighty secrets of the kitchen and of the pantry, as efficacious in their way as those Runic rhymes which could cleave mountains and shiver good steel swords.

We will, however, let her get to Hartford by herself, — it is a safe and easy journey, — while we communicate to the reader the experiences, indispensable to the understanding of the remainder of our tale, of Horace and Rachel in New York.

———

A great city is a great solitude. Within it, little settlements grow up here and there, as in a new country, of those who are neighbors by location, and who do or may become acquaintances or friends by intercourse. Sometimes these are established in some group of houses not very far apart from each other; sometimes the whole is included under one roof, like the nests of the sociable grossbeaks that we used to read about in the natural history.

These single-roof birds'-nests are sometimes found in boarding-houses; and it happened that our two Connecticut young folks drifted into one where, for the time being at least, all the birds in their little nests agreed. For it is too often that we see the shameful sight (we beg good Doctor Watts's pardon for imbedding one of his "inspired poems," as some admiring divine calls them, into our poor flat prose) of all the children of such a family falling out and chiding and fighting.

People in the city, again, and things in the city, are like those in the country, with the effects of density and excitement superadded. They are "fired up" very high by the sharp stimulus of their purposes and the further stimulus of the competition which makes every day a fight — not merely a struggle, but a fight — for life. They are magnetized, too, each by all the others. At night, from miles away on the Palisades or down the Bay, you can see a dusky red glare that caps the whole of the great city like a low-lying lurid cloud brooding down upon it. It is the generalized result and remainder of the millions of lights that are burning there, and that fill all the air above them with this red glow. Exactly such a lurid, dim, hot glow of mental and physical excitement incessantly broods over the city.

Now, the condition of things in which Horace and Rachel found themselves was a twofold state.

They underwent the excitement of New York, and were of course in more or less danger from it. Many of the places of abode which were suited to their means would for various reasons have concentrated and re-enforced this excitement and this danger. Even as it was, they did not escape entirely from it. It happened that certain countervailing influences, together with such resisting qualities as the two young persons possessed within themselves, saved them from any serious harm.

It was Rachel who had told Horace where to look for his city home.

" Come to Mrs. Worboise's with me," she had said. "I shall go there; and, if you don't like, then you can go away after a little while."

So he went. No danger that he should go away! Poor Mrs. Worboise! Her difficulty was, that she could not make people go away. As long as he staid in New York he abode with the plump, laughing, crying, soft-hearted motherly baby of a woman; and if he were to live there for centuries, he would never have thought of going away, nor for ten thousand years. Indeed, Jim Fellows, then a reporter, who was staying there at the time, used to shock the two serious boarders, Miss Doddle and Mrs. Pogey, every little while, by singing to the piano-forte in the parlor a naughty parody on a good Methodist camp-meeting hymn : —

When we 've been here ten thousand years,
   A stuffing just like fun,
Each greedy sinner will eat more dinner
   Than if he 'd just begun.

" You 'll surely be bankrupt, dame," Fellows would say. " No human being can set such a good table and take such care of boarders as you do and not be ruined."

And Mrs. Worboise would laugh her jolly, musical laugh, as cheery as a schoolgirl's, despite her fifty years and widowhood, and say, oh, she guessed not!

" But you know you will," persevered the teasing youth, on one of these occasions, not long after Rachel and Horace had enlisted under her banner: " how much does that pompous old Judge De Forest owe you now? Four hundred and fifty dollars, isn't it? "

" I do wish he would do something for me," said Mrs. Worboise, " that's a fact. He promises to pay half next Saturday, though."

" Mrs. Worboise," said Fellows, lifting his forefinger at the landlady in a stern and awful manner, " now answer me a straight question, upon your conscience and honor. Hasn't he made you that very promise every week for three months? — what? "

Poor Mrs. Worboise blushed as rosy as the evening clouds. She had one of those very fine, clear-tinted, transparent skins that never grow muddy nor rough, and her cheeks were as smooth as a plump little girl's, and she blushed as easily. Besides, she was caught. Fellows, a very perspicacious personage, had hit upon the exact nature of the Judge's financial relations with Mrs. Worboise: they had caused the poor landlady many a secret tear, and many an unconcealed one too, for that matter; for she cried at least as easily as she laughed. She laughed now; but there was a perceptible uneasiness in the laugh, and she said, with an effort, —

" Well, Mr. Fellows, if all my boarders were as honest and regular as you are, in spite of all your naughty words, I should get along very well."

" Naughty words, indeed ! " responded the young gentleman with a mighty affectation of anger. " I defy you to refer to a single improper-expression."

" But you are very irreverent, Mr. Fellows ! "

" That's only because I always say my prayers in secret, dame," — he almost always called her dame. " And you do take cheating so easily, that it's evident it's what you are for. It's a great shame that I don't cheat you; so it is. Do you know, Mrs. Worboise," he continued, suddenly changing his tone to one of embarrassment, " I am greatly troubled to raise some money to-day. Could you

possibly let me have fifty dollars until Saturday?
It would save me from real distress."

"Why, yes indeed, you dear boy!" cried out
Mrs. Worboise; and the tears stood in her great
soft brown eyes, ready to run over at his trouble;
"and more too. Here," — and she drew out a
pocket-book. "But remember Saturday; for indeed I must have it then: I have promised it on
the rent; and I 'm sadly behind."

She was eagerly counting out the bills; but Fellows burst out laughing, whereat she looked up in
the most innocent surprise imaginable, and saw
that she was deluded.

"Oh, that 's a shame!" she said. "You bad
man!"

"Yes," said the reporter gravely, "no doubt
you think so. That 's just like a woman. But
if you thought some of your money had been a
great help to me, nothing would make you think
me bad."

"Now, stop!" said the landlady. "Go along.
You know how much I like you. But I want
Rachel to help me now about some sewing; and
you must go away."

CHAPTER VII.

THE winter weeks fled rapidly away, their days and evenings crowded full and over-full of duties and of pleasures, all acting with strange new stimulus upon the clean and healthy but rural and inexperienced natures of Horace and Rachel. They were both of them finely organized, mentally as well as physically, both widely awake to whatever was about them, and sensitively impressible by it. Horace, moreover, possessed much more executive ability — *i.e.*, energetic good sense — than is at all usual or to be expected of people who have the gift of invention. Rachel, on her part, had more of the peculiar faculties which make a mechanic, than would have been expected of a woman, and particularly of one so very delicately fibred and of such introverted mental habits and almost excessively spiritualizing tendencies.

As for Horace, he was pretty well occupied by his book-keeping, by his own efforts at inventing, and by a course of study which he was very sensibly pursuing, in the principles of natural phi-

losophy and in the history of mechanics and invention. Still, he had a superabounding flow of life
and spirits; and it was with immense eagerness
and curiosity and keen enjoyment that he accepted all sorts of suggestions from master Jim
Fellows, to go and see, or go and help do, one
and another of the multifarious things and occur-
rences that a city reporter has to hunt up, or wit-
ness, or join in.

Rachel's situation was as similar to his, perhaps,
as a young woman's could be under the circumstances. She had not, it is true, such exacting
and peremptory and regular daily duties to drive
her, as those which bound Horace to stand at a
desk and compute and make entries so many hours
every day on pain of breach of contract, reprimand
from a stern employer, and angry expulsion from
a respectable and comfortably paid post. When
young women do have such external forces about
them, they train about as readily, perhaps, into
what are called "business habits," as young men;
but they seldom have them.

She was nominally making a winter's visit to
Mrs. Worboise, who was what may be called a
half-aunt. That is, Mrs. Worboise was half-sister
to Squire Holley; so that if she had had a daughter, such daughter would have been Rachel's half-
cousin; the two girls having in common only one

instead of two, out of their eight grandparents. Such relationships are the most convenient in the world. Brother and sister, or parent and child, are under a tremendous conventional imperative to be fond of each other, no matter how entirely unsuitable their tastes and feelings and views and pursuits may be. But half cousinships, for instance, and the like, can be made just as much or just as little of as you choose, and nobody thinks of saying a word.

Not that Mrs. Worboise was a person who took such things into account. Indeed, the dear little woman was an inexhaustible fountain of pure love and tenderness, which flowed forth upon good and evil almost as the Lord's warm sunshine falleth alike upon both. She had been for a long time coaxing Rachel to come and make her a visit; indeed, ever since the decease of her lord, the late Mr. Worboise, had, by a natural enough train of circumstances, launched her upon the troubled and perilous career of a New York boarding-house keeper's life — for which she was just as fit as any other little soft trustful baby would be to rule a gang of Apache Indians on horseback in all their war-paint and howls. So Rachel had delayed, and perhaps would never have come, had it not been for the explosion, as Nettie called it in her letter to Horace, which had tossed their little six-fold company in such diverse directions.

Rachel, although she had all those rarer beautiful qualities which belong to a young lady in a book, still, like most other people, had a good deal of human nature in her. She therefore in the course of time gradually recovered from that extreme grief which had overcome her at her mother's death. She began at once to go to church with Mrs. Worboise, who had been brought up a strict Calvinistic Presbyterian, and she was speedily snapped up by the enterprising Sunday-school superintendent, who happened to meet both the ladies together, as a teacher. She likewise dutifully attended the Thursday evening female prayer-meeting which was maintained with preternatural obstinacy by Mrs. Dr. Blewbly, the minister's wife, along with a few other of the sterner class of ladies, against the terrific onslaughts of Satan as he appeared in the guise of obstructions arising from city life. Mrs. Pogey and Miss Doddle were two of this earnest band; and Mrs. Worboise used to go regularly with them, because they took her, and Rachel used to go too, because Mrs. Worboise asked her.

Being as aforesaid a dexterous maiden, Miss Rachel quickly came into great request in the house in all things which have respect unto the cutting and fitting of dresses, and, indeed, in whatever pertains to the domain of needlework generally. She was already a pretty good workwoman on the sewing-machine, and she at once assumed the whole charge of all such matters for Mrs. Worboise herself, greatly lightening the toils of that overloaded and hard-working lady. Indeed, it was really only fair for her to insist upon remitting to Rachel the money which the latter tendered her at the end of a three-months' sojourn, aside from the fact that said sojourn was nominally a visit.

Then there were lectures or concerts or sights of some kind every evening. Then Miss Rachel had a course of reading too, no less than Horace; though it was one which some would judge not so useful. Indeed, that practical young gentleman grumbled a little in a careful manner, — for somehow he found himself very cautious about expressing any opposition to Rachel's more peculiar peculiarities — at the books she devoured so very eagerly. So would most of us perhaps. Yet, after all, it is pretty often true that the reading which we enjoy most does us most good. At any rate, other reading does not usually do us much good, for usually we won't read it. Rachel read eagerly a number of biographies and other works by and about mediæval and other mysticists; Jacob Bœhmen, Madame Guyon, and so forth. She worked through a good deal of Swedenborg. She tried a good many Spiritualist publications, but could not manage more than two or three of them; and she read industriously at a number of religious and serious periodicals which came to the house. And lastly, she adopted a shrewd suggestion of Horace's own. He, being a bit of a philosopher, though to tell the truth his dealings with Nettie did not always seem entirely philosophical, had a little theory about the faculties which constitute inventiveness; and he urged Rachel to try and see whether the same correct eye and hand that enabled her to fit a waist so accurately, and to judge so unerringly of sizes and proportions in cutting patterns and economizing materials, would not stand her in good stead in learning decorative design.

He had judged truly. The very suggestion of the Free School of Design at Cooper Union made her cheeks flush with delight. She went and returned home from her first attendance in a high state of pleasurable excitement. The superintendent said, she reported, that she did capitally; and she worked away, first with copies and so on, until she had mastered the handling of her pencil, and then, with constantly growing pleasure, in doing real work "from the round," and from original subjects; and in pursuance of another wise suggestion of Horace's she began therewith

to make herself acquainted as well as she could
with the history of her new avocation, finding
endless pleasure in it; most of all, by the way, in
tracing out those numberless connections and
interminglings of ornament and religion which
show such a necessary unison between the instinct
of beauty and the instinct of worship.

In all these pursuits of Rachel's, she was greatly
aided and abetted by a Mrs. Erling, who was
boarding in the house. Her husband was extant,
— which is not always the case with ladies' husbands in New York, — but he was hardly seen in
the house at all. He was an under-sized, blackish-
looking, dried-apple sort of man, a managing clerk
in a large law-office, very busy indeed, and, sooth
to say, about as little fitted to accompany his yoke-
fellow along the pathways which she preferred, as
could well be. He, however, like a man of sense,
made the best of it, let her have her own way, and
devoted himself wholly to his own affairs. He
hardly said a word at breakfast, shot off as soon as
it was over, and was never seen again at all until
next morning by anybody but his wife, unless he
chanced to be fallen in with about twelve o'clock
by some belated inmate, who discovered him un-
obtrusively entering by means of his night-key,
or silently gliding upstairs like an uncommonly
short, lean, and dark-complexioned ghost.

Mrs. Erling, however, was strangely different from him. She was a frail and almost translucent looking woman, still young, with a singularly pure and ethereal face, exceeding delicate in outline, very fair, with wonderfully limpid, soft eyes, which were surprisingly dark for one all whose other physical traits imported whiteness, and which therefore impressed you with the idea that they belonged to some one else.

She was every way such a person as you may fancy one of Baron Reichenbach's "sensitives" to have been, but without the positive sickness which seems to have been part of their professional outfit. Without being exactly a "Spiritualist," this Mrs. Erling was profoundly interested, and pretty well read, in the history — it has no philosophy yet — of that singular ghostly invasion (to admit for the moment its own claims) during the last quarter of a century which has chosen that name, and also in a great range of reading on related subjects, including the mystics already spoken of, remote inquiries about the earliest heretics and heretical sects, Gnostics and Manicheans, for instance, the purer heathen religions, magic, and so on. Rachel was naturally disposed to the wondering part of religious experiences, and of course found herself very ready to follow Mrs. Erling through her spiritual old curiosity shop.

4

At the same time, her whole religious training, and the naturally elevated tone of her own thoughts, kept her awake to the immeasurably superior purity, grandeur, and wonderfulness of Christianity. Thus, she was in no great danger from her forays into wonderland, though you could never have thought it, to listen to the heart-breaking lamentations of Miss Doddle and Mrs. Pogey, who were morally certain, and indeed stated in so many words, that Satan was evidently lying in wait for the young girl, and greatly desiring to have her, that he might sift her as wheat.

While time fled rapidly as aforesaid, other matters, without exactly fleeing, just went on as usual. Any of Mrs. Worboise's guests who chose, cheated her; and there were too many who did. Among these was old Judge De Forest, who was a disgraceful old humbug, not to put too fine a point upon it. He, as well as Horace, was an inventor, but of what, nobody seemed distinctly to know. He was a large, portly, red-faced man, very oily and voluble of speech, habitually talking of such astronomical sounding totals as millions of dollars, very energetic in wordy advocacy of all manner of what are called "advanced and reformatory" views; and he wore a frill to his shirt, chewed a good deal of tobacco in a rather juicy way, and walked with a gold-headed cane. He had some place or places which he called "of business," and he usually went to them. He spent a good deal of time, however, in his room, — he had one of the best rooms in the house, — at work at what seemed like mechanical drawing, with a big board, great sheets of white paper, pencils, and things; but at any hints respecting the said employment, he pursed up his mouth with great dignity, and assumed an air of haughty reserve quite wonderful to see, only intimating that it was impossible to discuss the higher secrets of science with ordinary folks.

Naturally enough, living so near together, and with so much that was in common in their ways of thinking, Horace and Rachel became more and more intimate, and more confidential and unreserved in exchanging thoughts. Rachel's unvarying sweetness of temper, and her unconscious unworldliness, diffused around her an atmosphere of rest which was exquisitely delightful to the young man, worried and as it were storm-tossed beyond expression as he had so often been with the turbulent unreasonableness of Nettie Sylva. His correspondence with this latter young lady, as may have been conjectured, had much the qualities after which Master Slender aspired in his proposed marriage relation with Miss Anne Page; there was no great love in the beginning (of the correspondence, of course), and it pleased Heaven to decrease it upon better acquaintance. It dwindled rapidly; and indeed quickly became practically extinct, yet without either amicable explanation or unkind word. The fact is, like the seed in the parable, because it had no root, it withered away.

So Horace waited on Rachel whenever she wanted an escort, and spent very many pleasant hours in reading or talking with her in the parlor or in Mrs. Worboise's own neat little sitting-room. She was as glad of his company as he was of hers; and he found a new and keen pleasure in seeing the dainty tact with which she used to manœuvre to escape from Jim Fellows or from the Judge, either as conversation-mate or escort, and to shelter herself under the wing of him, Horace. After some narrow escapes in such enterprises as these, from dilemmas which would have entailed either direct fibs or open refusals, Miss Rachel bethought herself of a device that is old enough, no doubt, but which Horace happened not to have thought of; and it gave him a degree of pleasure whose depth surprised himself. Perhaps there is no human bliss more inexpressible than that of him to whom a lovely woman unconsciously reveals that she prefers him. What Rachel pro-

posed was an engagement. Not *that*, reader;
another sort. It was a standing prior engagement
as escort; so that she might always say with truth
that she had to go with him.

CHAPTER VIII.

DID space permit, I should like to trace pretty fully the experiences of the year which Horace and Rachel thus spent in New York City. They were many and significant; for even so short a period as a year, during which we live broad, is evidently equal to a long one during which we live narrow, even on the principles of board measure. Mr. Tennyson has said very, much the same thing, in his terse maxim of comparative chronology about "fifty years of Europe" and "a cycle of Cathay." The thing is impossible, however; it would fill a book. The winter passed, and the spring came, with its abominably filthy streets, and the uprising again of all the evil smells that defile our greatest city. Dirtier fifty years of New York than a cycle of Cologne, I really believe. But the little band of pilgrims at Mrs. Worboise's boarding-house lived through it, although their landlady's delicately clean housekeeping probably made the streets worse to them than to anybody else. The months passed on; the

mud and smells of spring were succeeded by the
dust and smells of summer. But the discomforts of
the close and uncleanly city were often relieved by
the little excursions that Horace or Jim, — now
promoted, by the way, to an editorial post in the
office of " The Great Democracy," — used to organize at least once a week.; sometimes to Fort
Lee and the wooded summits of the Palisades;
sometimes to the heights of Staten Island above
the Narrows, where the dismantled old circular
sandstone tower of Fort Richmond stands in a
comatose state among the trees, or looking va-
cantly down upon the enormous modern water-
battery below. Sometimes they went over to
Greenwood; or rambled along the beach in the
vicinity of Fort Hamilton, — though the beauties
of the seashore thereabouts, and on Staten Island
as well, are too often profaned and ruined by the
sad remains of some defunct horse or dog, greatly
destructive of all romance. And the Central
Park was always open; a blessed parenthesis of
sweet air and wholesome nature let in among the
brick and stone, wholesome and refreshing as a
cool sleep between hot, weary days; Rachel and
Mrs. Erling particularly used to pass many a delightful half-day there; sometimes near the Mall
and the Lake and the shrubbery above it, sometimes in the less frequented and quieter regions at
the northern part of the Park.

The four quarters of the completed year went by; the cool nights of the last part of August foretold the coming of cool days in September, and in due time the cool days came. It was on one of these days that Horace, coming down to break-fast as usual, discerned upon the pleasant face of the landlady, obvious and unusually disfiguring traces of weeping. By this time Horace had estab-lished himself very strongly in the affections of Mrs. Worboise, who indeed had come to lean upon him very much as a widow does upon her grown-up son. She was fond of Jim Fellows, too, for the endless vagaries and quips of that rather fantastic person had a curious fascination for her. But she was rather afraid of him, or at least she never felt quite sure about him; while the more delicate tact and more respectful kindness of Horace had drawn her very near to him. It was therefore neither impertinent nor inquisitive for him to beckon her away from the breakfast-table a moment, before he departed to his business, and when she had accompanied him into the parlor, to ask her plainly what was the matter.

The poor little lady sat down on the sofa, and spoke. Horace was affected by her grief, for, as he said himself, he could scarcely help crying, tall, strong fellow as he was, when he saw the tears of another; and yet he could not help a sense of the ludicrous as Mrs. Worboise told her little story, her large soft eyes looking straight into his, and the tears coming out one after another close to her little pink nose, and pursuing each other down her soft cheeks until they fell into her lap, while so easily and fluently did she cry, that not a single sob interfered with her speech.

"O Horace! -I don't know what I shall do. I can't get any money from Mr. De Forest; and he owes me all by himself enough to pay almost a quarter's rent. And the landlord says he won't wait any longer; and if I don't pay up in full by the first of October, and a month in advance besides, he must have all my furniture as security, and I must leave the house on the first of November too. I suppose he ought to have his money; but it's very hard! I don't think he ought to take away every thing I have in the world!"

Now, Horace was what you may call a natural husband. That is, he had plenty of sense and energy, abundance of sympathy, and the proper tact of a man; which is, in cases like this, rather to support with fit encouragement than to add grief to grief.

"It's a great shame, Mrs. Worboise. But now, don't you feel bad until to-morrow, at any rate. I have something in my mind that will very likely help you. So cheer up, and keep up your courage.

4*

We 'll see you safe through, Providence permitting."

A little of this sort of general encouragement went a great way with such a facile and happy disposition. It was only a few moments before Mrs. Worboise felt a great deal better.

" There," she said, drying her eyes, "I 'm only a baby, after all. It 's very good of you, dear, to comfort me up: I won't feel bad any more, at least until you tell me I may. So now run away to your work."

Horace had an idea, it is true; one that he had considered a good many times; but if he had told Mrs. Worboise what it was, it would not have cheered her much, I fear. It does not sound like any thing very wonderful, — it was to see whether Jim Fellows couldn't be of some use.

But this was by no means so small a resource as you may think. A New York newspaper reporter, if he is smart and efficient, and what they call a rising man, and particularly if he is gifted with a small quantity of wickedness for extreme cases, can do a good deal. Horace and Jim walked down the street together, as they often did, and Horace opened the subject to him.

" Why, my son," responded Jim; "I 've been honing up the sword of justice for that old pig's throat this two months. Honor bright, is it, if I tell you?"

" Honor bright," said Horace.

" Well, then ; you know he owes the dame. now, after what deuced little he has ever paid, pretty near à thousand dollars. I 've worried about it some myself — you 've noticed that I grew thin and didn't eat any thing? "

" No," said Horace promptly.

" All right " (with a grin) ; " well, I had a notion three months ago that the old villain could pay if he chose, and I 've invested a little money to find out ; and I 've found out. I 've had him shadowed from time .to time ever since, but I 've not got quite all the facts I want yet. Am to see my man this very day ; will have the whole for you by tea-time. Meanwhile keep dark ! "

" I will. But, Jim, do you know what is it that the old fellow is inventing ? "

" No. Not my line."

" Well, I do. He 's been ordering a little job of iron work at our place, and he ordered some more of a fellow that I happen to know ; and I 've seen through that part of his tricks, anyhow. It 's a perpetual motion ! "

Jim, though no mechanic, had enough of general information and general incredulity together to let him laugh as easily as Horace himself at this idea.

" Why," resumed Jim, " I thought all those notions were dead."

" By no means; men are at work at such machines all the time.   I knew one myself, down
in North Greyford.   But I wonder Judge De
Forest should be such a fool.   He 's a swindler,
I don't doubt; but I don't see how he can swindle
anybody very deeply with such a bold imposition
as this."

" But I do, though!" said Jim.   " Why, Horace,
don't you see?   No, you can't; you don't know the
man he 's swindling.   Well, it 'll be safe enough
now, so I 'll tell you a little more, and you can put
that and that together.   I didn't know exactly what
his machine was, but I knew he was getting up a
machine.   And he has been receiving money to
pay for it, — and a good deal too, — a good deal
more than is necessary, by the same token, and
that 's just where the blessed old scamp means
to salt down a little *peculium* for himself."

" Well, but how can you work him so as to do
Mrs. Worboise any good?"

" Oh! you just leave your grandfather all alone
for that.   I 've got my little plans pretty near a
focus now.   I expected to touch him off soon;
but as you say you promised to comfort the dame
by this evening, I guess we can get the scenery
ready in season.   Well, here we are.   Hi-i-i-i!"
and he uttered an awful yell, just as they reached
the corner of Broadway, at which two young ladies

just before them jumped and squealed in a very delightful manner, and the omnibus driver, who was the person intended, turned round at once, though he was half a block away.

"See there!" said Jim; "so much for a pig's whisper: shot 'em flying, right and left. Well — *au reservoir!*" And he darted off, leaving Horace to go about his business.

At the boarding-house the hours went on but heavily; for the cheerfulness which Horace had inspired did not very long avail Mrs. Worboise against the steady, incessant weight of her money troubles. In the afternoon she coaxed Rachel to come and sit with her in her room. Rachel, as relative, friend, and helper, had grown to be even closer to the lonesome and loving-hearted little widow than Horace; closer, that is, in those exchanges of emotional expression and sentiment which, for want of husbands, husbandless women must be fain to transact with each other, since they are disclosures that will have secrecy, and if conjugal honor cannot be their shield, the honor of the sex must serve.

I need not reproduce the details of their discourse; the same inexorable fate, the abhorred fury with the shears, the Atropos of the printing-press, cuts short the thread of a story as remorselessly as her infamous old namesake the threads of lives; and I am compressed by mere violence into a summary of results. For the first time, Mrs. Worboise confessed plainly the hopeless state of her business affairs. So confidential had their relations been, that this may seem surprising; yet there must always be some last thing to confess, and with Mrs. Worboise this was it.

She admitted explicitly that she was absolutely incompetent to the horrid responsibilities of her post; but what was worse, she saw no prospect of any thing except losing all her furniture, — it represented a total of about two thousand five hundred dollars, less, of course, an important deduction for wear and tear, — and of being turned out of the only home she had, without a cent or a shelter.

It was a sufficiently melancholy picture, indeed; and as usual, Mrs. Worboise cried as she drew it. There was pretty sure to be water in all her landscapes. Rachel proceeded to pretty nearly repeat Horace's morning course of tonics. She ventured, indeed, a step farther than he had done; for she took the liberty of reproving her aunt, in a small feminine way, for not finding more comfort under her difficulties in her religion, — a sort of thing in reproofs very commonly to be observed in those youthful good folks who have not yet suffered any of the chronic and wearing afflictions which draw most heavily upon the religious constitution. After they have thus suffered, however, they find out what a labor it is to be happy by any means whatever, in circumstances which constitute unhappiness. But Mrs. Worboise had no disposition to answer in this sense. She was very meek, and confessed (with tears) that it was wrong; but that it was one of those times when every thing in the world seemed to be against her.

However, after a reasonable allowance of such healthful moral exercises, the two women grew a little more cheerful together, and then they fell to comparing of personal experiences; for nothing is so certain to bring out confidences, as confiding something. Here there came to the light mighty secrets, whereof, however, we shall refer to only two.

Mrs. Worboise hinted that she had expected Rachel would be at once Mark Hinsdale's wife and her father's housekeeper; in reply to which Rachel, in a quiet, serious way, intimated that perhaps it might have been so, but that Mark had greatly distressed her, and, she thought, done wrong, in pressing her as earnestly as he did to marry him while her grief was so fresh at her mother's death; and that in consequence the currents of their feelings about each other had quite changed. Then Mrs. Worboise intimated further that perhaps

Horace, &c. To which the demure Rachel only
said, — hardly blushing, and with proper and ac-
curate caution in utterance, — that he hadn't asked
her, — a very safe answer. Then Mrs. Worboise
replied that he meant to, — she knew it, she said,
— putting a thought too much emphasis on her
verb; upon which Miss Rachel dexterously turned
the conversation, and talked away famously about
Uncle Worboise.

But whether or not they did each other any other
good, at any rate they got rid of nearly all the afternoon; insomuch that before they knew it, it was
time to get ready for tea.

CHAPTER IX.

TEA came, and the boarders came to tea. Nothing has been said in this history, as nothing was needed, — and there was no room if any thing had been, — about the rank and file of this noble army. Suffice it to observe, that they filled a pretty long table in the large basement dining-room, which had been carried through into the original kitchen of the house; that having, in its turn, been driven out into an addition built upon part of the back yard. Judge De Forest was present with his frill and his dignity; Miss Doddle and Mrs. Pogey were there with their serious and improving observations, — what a pity that it is out of the question to transfer a seasoning at least of their discourse into these comparatively frivolous pages! — Rachel was there, and Horace, and Mrs. Erling, and Jim Fellows, the scandalizing tease, who used to vex the righteous souls of those two saintly women, to startle Mrs. Worboise, and to amuse Rachel and Horace and himself, with deftly chosen observations, which seemed awfully irreverent at first; but which he always defended in such a manner as to confound, if not convince, his opponents, who at last came to treat him mostly with that peculiar sort of tender consideration which a puppy learns to display in nosing a chestnut-burr. Jim, by the way, according to the etiquette in such cases, briefly introduced this evening to Mrs. Worboise a quiet and respectable-looking man, whom he named as Mr. Crafts; a professional acquaintance, he observed, whom he had taken the liberty of inviting to sup with him. Mrs. Worboise accordingly received Mr. Crafts, and seated him next Jim, with her wonted kindly courtesy; though Horace and Rachel, if not the others, saw that she was still distraught with her troubles, no matter how bravely she strove to thrust them down out of the way of her official duties. And the viands of the meal were served, and there were chat and pleasantry and laughter as usual.

" Thank you for the toasted codfish," observed Master Jim to his *vis-à-vis*, Mrs. Pogey. " Dreadful thing, if they only knew it, to be grilled so after they 're dead, — hay ? "

Mrs. Pogey groaned and shook her head, and answered,—

" Mr. Fellows, if we sin against great light we shall no doubt find a dreadful fate awaiting us after death."

"Light?" replied Jim, as cheerfully as if the good lady had made the most humorous suggestion in the world — "light? Codfish ain't much on optics. Hefty in acoustics, though, — all tongues and sounds inside. Ever listen to one of those sounds? Gung'l, the fiddler, was a Newfoundlander; did you know that, Mrs. Worboise? So fond of sounds that he always kept a keg of 'em by him to smell at for inspiration in composing. Named his very best set of waltzes after it — '*Sounds* from home,' you know."

Then he looked across to the Judge, who was solemnly imbibing his Oolong, and continued, "By the way, Judge, how comes on the perp?"

Judge De Forest started, set down his cup, and looked across with a most severe and deeply offended air.

"-Etual," insisted Jim, with a wink. "Oh, we know a thing or two, Judge! No hyphens between friends, Judge. But that wasn't what I was going to say. Any sounds from *your* home recently, Judge?"

The old fellow's face grew quite purple with heavy wrath and dignity.

"Mr. Fellows," he remarked, in his most judicial manner, "I fail to apprehend either the significance or the propriety of your observations, sir. They are unseasonable, sir. I fear that you have

been somewhat thoughtless in your use of stimulat-
ing liquors, sir. You are certainly violating the
proprieties, sir!"

Jim opened his mouth to reply, when a sharp,
high, female voice broke in, —

"Jedge, indeed! Not haaf so much as you're
a violatin' on 'em this minnit, Ephraim Huggins!"

"Oh!" cried Mrs. Worboise, "I forgot to in-
troduce Mrs. Huggins!"

Then she stopped short; in fact, it *was* a super-
fluous introduction. The silence that followed
was, for a moment, perfect. Then a single *sniz-
zling* giggle *would* squeeze out through Jim Fellows's teeth, though he held in as hard as he could.
Horace, seeming to understand, managed to laugh
silently; and the stranger, Mr. Crafts, too, smiled;
a kind of grim smile, that intimated amusement
rather than surprise. But the blank, ineffable
astoundment of all the rest can hardly be dreamed.
As for the Judge, nothing can do justice to his
bearing except, perhaps, a horrid picture that I
once saw of a monstrous old bison being worried
to death by a gang of prairie wolves; blinded,
bleeding at a hundred wounds, helpless to reach or
to escape his agile assailants, resisting, indeed, only
in the vast mass of his slow enduring vitality. So
the heavy old judge, thus beset, still maintained
his pompous manner; though a very close observer

might have noticed even a kind of tremor during the *impromptu* observations of the high-voiced lady; and there assuredly was a shade of uncertainty in his tones when he responded, and he would not look towards the lady aforesaid, who had jumped up when she began her apostrophe, and remained standing. All the rest could thus perceive that she was oldish, thin, and indeed skinny; pale and worried-looking, with thin lips, a cross expression, a peaked, red-tipped nose, scanty hair, and a shabby old dress. Perhaps if they had known her as well as the Judge, they would not have looked at her any more than he did. She certainly was not pretty to see, as she stood there quivering with nervous excitement, and her little, pale, watery eyes looking venomously at the august object of her ire. The Judge arose, and it was to Mrs. Worboise that he spoke:—

"Madam, I have been grossly insulted at your table. I shall withdraw, madam. I am by no means accustomed to such treatment, and shall not put up with it, madam!"

And, pushing back his chair, he left the room without attending to the embarrassed apology which Mrs. Worboise began to offer. Even before the door closed behind the burly frame of the Judge, however, Mr. Crafts arose with much nimbleness, and, without a word of apology or explana-

tion, darted out after him. Jim and Horace
followed, rather more deliberately. Mrs. Huggins sat down. All the rest of the boarders looked
at each other in a stunned sort of way, and
exchanged expressions of wonder in low tones.

In a moment Jim looked in, and asked Mrs.
Worboise to be good enough to step into the par-
lor a moment. She did so, and found the unhappy
Judge again at bay.

" O Mr. Fellows ! *pray* tell me what does it all
mean ? " she cried out, in a terrible state of flut-
ter.

" Just what I asked you in here for," observed
he. " But take a seat. We 'll finish our negotia-
tions in a moment. What is the whole amount
due you from Huggins ? "

" You mean Judge De Forest ? " asked Mrs.
Worboise timidly.

" No more a judge than yourself, madam,"
broke in Crafts sententiously. " Ephraim Huggins of Saint Louis, State of Mizzoorah, spekila-
ter."

With a good deal of difficulty the good lady, at
Jim's reiterated demand, and with wide, scared
eyes, managed to get enough of her wits together
to fix on the correct sum total, — a little short of
nine hundred dollars. Fellows summarily said,
" We 'll call it the round sum ; little enough for

interest;" and he scribbled a receipt in full, and laid it before Mrs. Worboise, saying, —

"Sign that, please."

"But"—she began, naturally enough—

"All right, marm," said Crafts.

"Yes," assented Horace, "it's right; do, Mrs. Worboise." And she signed, like one in a dream.

"There," said Jim: "check for that amount, Huggins, if you please."

"Suppose I won't, what then?" said Huggins surlily.

"Take him, Crafts," said Jim; "we won't have a particle of nonsense."

Crafts now showed and read an order of arrest on a charge of swindling, and sued out in behalf of one Marcus Wendall.

Huggins, at hearing this name, muttered a pretty large oath, and without a word took out a big fat pocket-book, drew from it a blank check, filled and signed it, and pushed it over the table.

"No go," said Jim, who read it carefully. "*T'other bank*, Huggins!"

Evidently with the very bitterest reluctance, the detected swindler substituted another check.

"There, Mrs. Worboise," said Jim, "there's your money. But do you be sure and cash the check the moment the bank's open to-morrow. If Crafts had let the old villain get out of the front

door he was pointing for when he left the table,
you wouldn't have got it.   I reckon we've got to
keep him here all night as 'tis, and Crafts along
with him, to make it a sure thing — that is, unless
he wants to sleep in the station-house, and also,
unless Mrs. Worboise orders him into the street."

"Oh, no!" she cried out. "Oh, not in the
least!"

"Or," suggested Crafts, in his grimmest manner,
"unless the old gentleman'd like the society of
his lawful wife."

Even Huggins appeared to see that this was not
a serious suggestion.   It was therefore agreed that
Mr. Crafts should be intrusted with the pleasing
task of watching over the slumbers of Mr. Huggins, in place of that fairer companion whom he
seemed to scorn.

"Well," said Huggins, "if you're through with
me, I am with you; I'll go upstairs."

"Wait a moment," said Horace, — "Here, Jim."
They conferred a moment in a corner. "Good!
first-rate!" exclaimed Jim. "Call 'em in."

Horace stepped out, and brought in Rachel and
Mrs. Huggins.   Rachel sat down close to Mrs.
Worboise, and Mrs. Huggins opposite her lord.

"Mrs. H.," said Jim, "we've been thinking
that perhaps it would do nicely all round if our
friend there should just hand you half his cash

balance now in bank, and then you leave him alone again! That 'll give you — let 's see " — he took out a memorandum — " about thirteen hundred dollars."

Mrs. Huggins considered a moment, and consented.

" That is," suggested the practical Crafts, " until you find out that he 's got another amount to levy on."

Wincing, if any thing, more than before, the victim drew another check, and was then allowed to depart under the charge of the vigilant Crafts to his own room. Jim renewed to Mrs. Huggins, who was also going upstairs, the caution he had given to Mrs. Worboise about the check; and then Mrs. Worboise insisted that Jim Fellows should tell her what she had been about, and what he had been about: " For, mercy me! " exclaimed the puzzled landlady, " I feel as if I had been whirled round in a coffee-roaster! "

Jim explained. He told the landlady how he had been watching Huggins for a long time; how he had only this very day found out about two bank-accounts, the sham and the true; how the vengeful Mrs. Huggins had a few days ago come to New York in search of her recreant lord, and going to the detective head-quarters, had fallen in with Crafts, who had forthwith notified Jim, and

5   G

thereupon the tea-table tableau had been blocked out.

" But what made him do as you told him to ? " asked Rachel.

" Why, bless you, didn't you see the order of arrest ? " asked Jim.

" But what has he done to Wendall ? "

" Got a lot of his money. But the real thing that frightened him was, that I let him know I would expose him in the papers in full, in my most picturesque style, if he didn't pay up. That would have broken up his whole arrangement with Wendall."

" Why," said Horace, " broke it up ? Wendall has sued out this order of arrest now.".

" No, he hasn't," said Jim coolly. " When the ladies have got their money, I shall notify Huggins that the warrant is all a hum, and that he can proceed against me for false imprisonment or conspiracy or forgery or high treason, if he wants. He 'll be as still as a mouse, though, no fear of that."

" Why," said Horace again, his eyes wide open, " it 's a forgery ! "

" No ; the statute defines that," calmly explained Master Jim. " I asked a lawyer. It 's a misdemeanor ; but we 'll burn the *corpus delicti* in good season ; and the recording angel will blot out the entry with a tear, as he did Uncle Toby's oath because I'm a good little boy, after all."

It was a fact; the reckless fellow had certainly perpetrated a legal offence, and a pretty serious one; yet it was so extremely fine a specimen of poetical justice, that one can hardly help being glad afterwards, though none of us could really have recommended it in advance.

Mrs. Worboise intended to transfer the whole of her money to the landlord. But Jim and Horace, acting a good deal like joint conservators for her benefit, forbade this, saying that half of it was quite enough.

"Fact is," said Jim, "I know you can't go on here, dame, just as well as you do, and a sight better too. You ought to put the money in your pocket and leave."

Here a servant brought in a letter for Rachel, saying that it had fallen down behind the table on which the carrier's letters were laid at the afternoon delivery, and that she had just found it on the floor. Rachel read it, and handed it to Mrs. Worboise. It was from Squire Holley, and was an urgent request to his half-sister to close up her New York business and come and keep house for him.

"He's just as good as he can be," said the landlady tearfully. "I don't know what to say."

"I do," said Horace. "I'll bet that sly thing told her father to do that!"

Rachel blushed. "Well," said she, "if I did, it was in good season, wasn't it? Mayn't I help Aunt Delia as well as you?"

"Surely," said Horace; "and very good of you to do it. And Mrs. Worboise must go too. Now, Mrs. Worboise, cash your check in the morning. Jim and I will go and see Mr. Warren this very minute."

Warren was the landlord. The young men went instantly. He was a sufficiently well-disposed old fellow, but would not give them much of an answer that night, saying — very naturally — that he must see his tenant.

However, within a few days an arrangement was made by which Mrs. Worboise's lease was surrendered; her furniture and carpets, which under her skilful and diligent management were in remarkably good order, were appraised; the landlord knew of a lady, he said, who would, he thought, take charge of the whole establishment at the end of September; and not only was Mrs. Worboise able to retain the whole of her money from Huggins, but there was a little surplus due her from the furniture, over and above the arrears of rent which it paid for.

Notice was given to the boarders accordingly;

and on or before the 30th September, 1871, they either searched out other homes, or arranged to remain under the new administration.

As for Huggins, he departed on the morning after his exposure, with his frill much rumpled, his feathers generally in a very draggled state, and his bank-account horribly dilapidated. He talked big to the very last, assuring Crafts that he should hear from him.

CHAPTER X.

THE diligent reader has already learned that Nettie Sylva and Jeff Fleming found their way to the ancient and wealthy city of Hartford. It is such a trifle to travel nowadays, that I need only say that they went at such times as pleased them, by rail, from Greyford to New Haven, and thence to Hartford. Nettie's Aunt Helen lived in a little cosey tenement of her own, in the southern part of the city; and Nettie went, of course, to her home. As for Jeff Fleming, he established himself at first in a hall bedroom, and "lived in his trunk;" but being at once independent and sociable in his tastes, he quickly devised a scheme which was on many accounts much more agreeable; and enlisting two or three decent young fellows, a clerk in the same store with him, and others, acquaintances of the same clerk, they found some empty rooms all in a row on the upper floor of a great building all full of offices, in the heart of the city, and, buying cheap new carpets and sets of furniture, they fitted up a very nice little colony in the air, — three little bedrooms, and a fourth room for a parlor. Here they lived in great mirth and harmony; for though no two of them were alike, yet that only made the quartet more entertaining to its members; and, as they were all manly and well-meaning young men, they were in no danger of jars or disagreements.

It is a pity not to acquaint you with the fun and jollity those four had in "the dove-cot," as they christened it, and of the serious communion too; for thorough good fellows like these four will be sure to discuss as they go along together both the funny and the serious sides of every thing. As for Jeff, he was a sociable, organizing, and suggestive person, full of ideas, and greatly inclined to set them forth; in danger therefore, if in any danger in that direction, of becoming wordy and long-winded. Jerry Bigelow was full of puns and verbal jocularities; and he therefore tended to his own proper sort of tediousness. Punsters, however, have to be quick-witted; and thus they well know that the sole condition on which they are tolerated is, that they endure the pick-pocket similitude, and all manner of other snubbing and reprobation usually, of course, administered by persons not bright enough to do what they affect so greatly to despise; so that the pretty uniform course of ingenious discouragements which his three com-

panions provided for him no more discouraged
Master Jerry than the jeers and sarcasm of the
heathen would a pious and enthusiastic mission-
ary. Ralph Van Orden was neither a joker nor a
talker. He was handsome, dark-faced, a little slow
of speech, and a fine singer of many songs and bal-
lads, which he accompanied, by ear, on the guitar.
Last of the four was Abram Wilks, a tall flaxen-
haired fellow, slender even to lankness, awkward
and queer as possible, with a great taste for collec-
tions of all kinds, — shells, coins, old books, eggs,
any thing that could be classified or even put in a
row.

Jeff's circle of friends began to enlarge before he
had been many weeks in Hartford. In a town like
that, crowded with an immense concentration of
business, there is a gathering of both young men
and old almost as busy and wide-awake as in
enormous New York. At the same time, the very
fact that the city is small prevents the sense of
loneliness that springs up amid the New York
multitude, and preserves a portion of the feeling of
guardianship and watchfulness by the community
over the individual. This is a wonderfully valuable guarantee of decency and uprightness in life.
So Jeff flourished and made progress with great
speed ; became an active member of the Sons of
Temperance, and of a debating society connected

with the Young Men's Institute ; a diligent and
inquisitive scholar in a Bible-class at the Centre
Church Sunday-school, sometimes even somewhat
to the bewilderment of the intelligent but rather
conventional gentleman in charge ; a useful member of the choir — for Jeff sung a very fair bari-
tone, and could even serve as a tenor in case of
great necessity, with a little strain or even a falsetto
on a few of the higher notes, and constant care to
sing in a head voice.

As for Nettie Sylva, her case was about equally
fortunate. Her aunt was much older than Dr.
Sylva ; and having always had an especial fond-
ness for Nettie, the relation between them was
more like the loving tenderness of affectionate
grandparent and grandchild, than a mere ordinary
collateral kinship in the second degree. Aunt
Helen was quite an old lady, wearing her own gray
hair under a neat cap, always dressing in black or
gray, precise and rigid in all her views, feelings,
and sentiments, and especially high and unbending
in respect of goodness of family, belonging in this
as well as in some other respects to a class of which
but few specimens are nowadays left, like lofty
peaks of a primitive formation, rising through the
homogeneous " tertiary drift " and " recent allu-
vium " of our average communities. Her husband,
Deacon Tarbox, was a dry and quaint old gentle-

5*

man, with the oddest prim air about him, and of a
precision, conservatism, orthodoxy, and careful cor-
rectness generally, of such inexpressible rigidity,
that in comparison with him, even poor strict
Aunt Helen might appear quite randy. But he
had a good deal of humor of a high and dry sort,
which he dealt out sparingly, and with something
like an air of regret, as a miser dislikes to see coin
move away from his fingers, irrespective whether
gain or loss is to follow.

Deacon Tarbox and Aunt Helen always had
baked beans for supper Saturday night, and the
same cold for dinner on Sunday, the latter meal
being sometimes re-enforced by a dish of cold
meat and invariably by pie and a cup of tea.
Jeff had called to see Nettie very soon after they
came to Hartford; and the young man, having had
the tact to keep pretty much all of his ideas to himself, and to assent to whatever was suggested by the
seniors in the way of doctrines, whether secular or
theological, became highly acceptable in their eyes.
His membership of the Bible-class and of the choir
— as it happened it was at the Centre Church that
Mr. Tarbox was deacon — confirmed this good opinion, as did also his co-operation in the temperance
reform; and thus it fell out that not only was Jeff
installed as Nettie's usual escort to rehearsals — she
sang alto, by the way, and a good alto too, — on

Saturday evenings; but it came to be the recognized order of events, that he should take tea at Deacon Tarbox's Saturday evenings, and should also, whenever he chose, be allowed to walk home with the family from church, and partake of the modest and cool but substantial regulation dinner of that day. It need not be said that at these sabbath occasions — Deacon Tarbox always said "the sabbath," and never "Sunday" — the greatest seriousness of word and look was a matter of course. But Jeff Fleming, a New England boy, knew this well enough; no danger of his offending in this respect, so long as he should wish to preserve the good opinion of the deacon, or to be even tolerated within his gates. It is possible that this rigid law was slightly relaxed during the Saturday evening after sunset; but the difference, if there was any, was but a shade. It was the old school of observances as well as of theology to which Deacon Tarbox belonged, and had belonged from his youth up, and in which he would continue to his death, should that be a thousand years hence.

The first occasion, however, on which Jeff was admitted to the deacon's hospitality, was a weekday one, only a few days after his arrival, and before he was quite settled in his new home; being a dinner, to which he was invited by Aunt Helen so very pressingly that he could not well refuse. He must stay, really, said the good old lady; she did not see Greyford faces every day, and his mother was her father's second cousin.

In the matter of kinship, the Yankees are al-most as tenacious as the Scotch; and those of the country towns especially. It belonged to the quiet and steadfast character of Aunt Helen to preserve this sentiment, even after her many years' residence in the busy city; and Jeff respond-ed to it with the vivacious pleasure of a youth who finds unexpected friends. However, the chief reason for recording this first dinner was not so much its being a demonstration of natural affec-tion, as the fact that it gives an opportunity to chronicle one of Deacon Tarbox's characteristic sayings. If the occasion had been Sunday, or Saturday evening either, he would have bitten his own head off before he would have said it; be-sides that the subject-matter would have been absent. They had a roast pig for dinner on the day in question, succulent and toothsome enough to have inspired the famous treatise of Charles Lamb on the subject, and which pleased well the healthy young appetites of Miss Nettie and Mas-ter Jeff. The young gentleman, indeed, expressed his approbation in warm terms, and asked Aunt Helen how she could possibly contrive to produce such a marvellous triumph of the culinary art.

Before the old lady could say whatever she meant
to say, her quaint old husband answered for her,
with his very driest manner, in his most precise and slow utterance, with an extra portion
of solemnity about his prim, thin lips, and with
a funny, formal bow across the table to his
spouse : —

"I will tell you, Mr. Fleming. She always
gets into the oven along with the roast."

Of course when the winter came down the
broad Connecticut River Valley all the way from
Canada, ice followed, and smoothed out all his
footsteps upon lake and stream. Jeff and his
three friends, being at that happy age when the
puzzle of life is how to expend the surplus of it,
hastened to overhaul their skating tackle, and to
use whatever spare hours they could command, in
staying out in the cold and scratching about on
the ice. As the march of mind had not omitted
Greyford, so Nettie had learned to skate ; and
Jeff and she had some very nice excursions on the
broad and glassy surface of the Connecticut, during a "cold snap" of a week or two, before snow
came. Sometimes the four young men went together ; and once or twice a party of eight was
organized, each escorting his steel-shod damsel.
All this mirth and jollity, however, and other
agreeable things too, were brought to a sudden

close, by no less an event than the loss—or at
least the irreparable injury—of a tall or stove-
pipe hat, and the consequences thereof, which be-
fell as here followeth.

One blowing Saturday afternoon, when the early
closing movement had enabled Jeff to take an extra number of hours' skating, as if to get himself
well stiffened up about the legs for Sunday, Nettie
and he went down to the river as usual to skate.
They got safely out upon the ice, fastened on
their skates, and went careering about up and
down before the docks and all along the city front.
As the afternoon advanced, and it drew towards
evening, the dull, gray clouds seemed to thicken;
the north-wester, which had been raving along the
river all the afternoon, whisking into small drifts
and winrows a little dry snow that had fallen
within a day or two, seemed to grow stronger and
stronger, instead of lulling as sunset approached;
and whistled and whewed along out from under
the heavy, lumbering mass of the "Great Bridge,"
with such a vengeance that it really required a
good deal of pluck as well as muscle to make
head against it.

Nettie and Jeff had more than once made their
way defiantly up to the bridge, in the very teeth
of old Boreas, (was he north-west?) and then,
turning, had spread out their arms like sails, and

glided victoriously forth, literally upon the wings of the wind, far away to the south; standing perfectly still, and borne over the smooth ice as swiftly and steadily as two great birds in the air.

What it was that made Jeff· Fleming wear a tall hat out into that frozen hurricane, it is useless to conjecture. Why, indeed, he wore one at any time, or why any human being should do so, unless compelled by the sentence of a court of justice, as Chinese felons go about with a thick plank round their necks, I for my part cannot imagine. If the young man had known — but how fortunate for people who write about such circumstances that the persons in question do not know ! .At any rate, Jeff usually wore a tall hat, and with masculine obstinacy he wore it now. By means of the most energetic jerks he had seated it so firmly on his head that it might well have been believed capable of removal only "with it, or on it," like a good Spartan and his shield. But there is, as some philosopher has profoundly observed, an "innate depravity of inanimate matter." This, probably, imperceptibly loosened the hat. The really tremendous cold, in spite of Jeff's young blood and vigorous exercise, had, moreover, begun to drive the feeling out of his forehead, and to substitute the cold numb band next the hat-rim, which the votaries of the abominable thing know all about, and which prevented him from knowing that it was becoming loose. Perhaps, too, for there are absolutely no exceptions, we are told, to the operations of the great natural laws, the cold was contracting his head a little — who knows? At any rate, just as they swept swiftly down to the end of one of their long, southwardly trips, and whirled round to fight their way back again against the vengeful north-wester, off went Jeff's hat, and bowled away down the river, skipping along and turning this way and that as if it were alive and looking round with one great empty eye to see if anybody were coming after it. Jeff flung up one hand as quick as lightning, but too late. Prompt in deciding, and not able to afford to lose a nice new hat, he merely cried out to Nettie, "Don't wait — I'll catch up!" and sprang forth after the fugitive.

Nettie stood laughing a moment, to see the fun, but it was too cold to stand. Turning about, she struck out with long, resolute strokes, for the bridge, and in a few seconds was out of sight round a low woody point.

Twice or thrice Jeff all but caught his fleeing head-gear; and once, as it lodged for a moment in a light snow-wreath, he even stooped to lay hands on it. But — as he afterwards said in describing the experience — it "laughed right in his face,

and hopped off again." It bounded and rolled,
shooting across broad glassy spaces, vaulting with
diabolic nimbleness over any little impediment,
until the enraged proprietor almost thought he
could see an imp riding inside of it, and making
impertinent gestures backward at him over the
rim. His ears quickly began to tingle, and then
to lose their feeling, and he had to rub them furiously more than once. Even the very top of his
head, through all his thick hair, began to feel the
sharp bites of the relentless icy wind. Angrier
than ever, he gathered his strength, filled his
lungs full, set his teeth, and, though he was already
flying along under the double impulse of legs and
tempest at a rate that a locomotive could hardly
have matched, he darted forward for one final
spurt —

And with barely time for a cry, he flew with a
monstrous plunge away down into the deep, dark
blue waters of Connecticut River, rushing, with
the tremendous momentum of his speed, twenty
feet beyond the furthest edge of the thinning
transparent black ice, that he had seen for the
merest instant beneath his feet, infinitely too late
for even an effort to save himself, and hardly long
enough, so lightning-quick was the motion, to
know that he was gone.

CHAPTER XI.

WHILE Jeff is paddling about in the water, let us make a few calm observations. We are better situated for that purpose than he, although he may have the advantage of us in point of coolness. What he soused into was not what is called an " air-hole ; " it was a broad strip of open water, stretching across the whole width of the river, just at a turn in the channel, and where a sort of ripple caused by some bar or obstruction at the bottom had thus far resisted all the powers of Jack Frost. If this hat-chase of his had been foreseen, any of his Hartford-bred friends would have cautioned him about this bend in the river. If it had not been half-dark, and if he had not been so vexed and eager about his hat, or if he could possibly have imagined the existence of any such hole — in short, if for any reason whatever Jeff had not done it, it would not have been done. But he did ; and there he is, at last, scrabbling and slopping in that mush of ice .and water that is working and rustling along the edge of the river in the very innermost elbow of the bend. Instantaneous as his plunge had been, and amazing as it was, Jeff was too practised a swimmer not to shut his mouth tight as he went under; and he was too ready and too strong to be either terrified or paralyzed in mind or body, as a feebler person or a less experienced aquatic would have been. So, without trying to free himself from either skates or overcoat, he half instinctively felt the truth, that in that freezing water no man could live móre than minutes; and that if he got out at all, it must be at once. No man who has not passed through some such peril understands what efforts can be condensed into seconds, where the jaws of death are even closing over him. But the usefulness of many a long run on land and many a long swim in the sea now showed itself. Even if years of life had been drained in that awful struggle of two minutes, the victory was cheap. Despite the skates (it seemed as if his feet weighed a thousand pounds); despite the weight of his heavy water-soaked clothing, he got his face above water; at one look saw the shore, and went rushing for it with desperate leaps, throwing himself along edge-ways, shoulder first, not able to surge his body above the water to the waist, as he had often done in the summer waters of the Sound, but yet deci-sively mastering the cold, cruel, lapping flood.

He struck wet clay, both with knee and hand, just as breath and strength began to fail together. No human being can put forth his very uttermost of strength or motion except for just so long as he can hold his breath. Eagerly enough he scrambled and slopped his way out, clutching ice, mud, leaves, sticks, whatever lay along that soiled and dreary margin. His laden feet sank and stuck in mire; he was bedaubed with the blue-gray clay from head to foot; but he had escaped the deadly river!

However, it was only to encounter a second foe no less deadly. Prompt and ready as ever, he forced his way up the frozen slope of the steep bank; sat down instantly, while his hands should retain some life, and tried his skate-straps. He could not bring his numbing fingers to bear. He took out his pocket-knife, opened it with his teeth, and cut the straps. Already, since he came out of the water, the skates had frozen tight to his feet, and he only knocked them off with a desperate kick. Then the idea came into his mind that it would be a very easy thing for him to freeze to death, there on the farther side of the river, though within plain sight of thousands of the city's twinkling lights. And — as it always will be with some minds — he thought of it as at once horrible and absurd; and he smiled, though his teeth were chattering fearfully.

"I've no hat, either!" he said to himself. But he did not sit still for all this, by any means. It was all in his mind in a flash. As he threw off his skates, he sprang up, his overcoat crackling and stiff already; picked the skates up, thrust one into either coat pocket, and turning north-ward up the river, set out on a full run. But as the wind met him, it seemed to craunch his face and his head too, all over, all at once, with some-thing that, as he thought, felt more like red-hot iron than arctic cold. It was again a question of minutes; perhaps Jeff was in no less danger than he had been when under water. But he stopped short, tore off the coat, drew it together over his head, leaving just room for one eye to peep out, and once more struck into a vigorous run. It was useless to consider whether he could get home. He *must* run, until he could run no more, unless he reached help before his running was exhausted.

He had gone perhaps a quarter of a mile, shel-tered somewhat for part of the way by a thin growth of willows, and, fortunately, finding but few fences to climb over, when, as he ranged up opposite the great Arms Factory, he began to feel that he had not running enough left in him to get up opposite the heart of the city and so on to his rooms. There were no houses in sight on his side of the river; for all the land is meadow, flooded deep in the high spring freshets; nor any road, nor living thing.

"There's just one thing to do," reflected Jeff. "I'll cross here and make straight for Aunt Helen's."

No sooner said than done. He turned short, ran down the bank, here sloping and sandy, hurried out upon the river, not without a sort of horror of it, crossed over, climbed the dyke, made his way up the first cross-street, and after asking the road of half a dozen different citizens, all of them scared enough, to be accosted by an apparently headless apparition, like a pedestrian Brom Bones, and all icy and crackling as it hurried along, he rang furiously at the door of Deacon Tarbox's snug mansion.

The deacon himself opened it.

"Please let me in!" said poor Jeff, not very ready with his etiquette at the moment.

"Who are you?" demanded the startled deacon, — not so brave in mere physical matters as in those of conscience. But it was not the custom to refuse charity at that house, though it was not the custom to administer it at the principal entrance.

"Who are you? Go round to the back-door." And partly irritated at what he conceived to be the presumptuousness of the applicant, and a little dismayed withal by the uncouthness of this goblin, with its one eye peeping out through the opening of the coat, he drove the door to with a most peremptory and undeacon-like slam.

Half dead as he was, Jeff laughed within himself as he dragged himself round the corner of the house — for, as is natural, having now reached succor, the effect of the tremendous strain which his frame had undergone began to come down upon him with a suddenness that he did not at all understand. He reached the back-door, however, just as the deacon opened it with a rather stern —

" This iŝ the proper door for " —

He did not finish his sentence. As he opened the door, a tall figure swayed gently forward against it, then toppled over against him, and slid down to the floor, crackling somewhat, in a heap.

" Dead drunk! " muttered the deacon to himself, with disgust and horror ; and his first thought was to bundle the beggar-man out upon the steps and shut the door. Then the deacon bethought him of the fearful cold of the weather; he had kept a daily thermometrical and meteorological record for fifty years in that very house ; and considering that a few seconds more or less was nothing to the victim of King Alcohol, he stepped to a window close by, just outside of which hung his record thermometer, and inspected it through the glass.

" Whew ! " whistled the old deacon to himself,
— " fifteen degrees below ! He wouldn't last long
out there ! "

And setting down his lamp, with reluctant hands,
and a face puckered into lines of contemptuous
abhorrence enough for at least one hundred ordinary deacons, Deacon Tarbox bent over the person
on the floor, and essayed to draw the coat from his
face. The first time he let go in astonishment.

" Why, it 's frozen as stiff as an oak plank ! "

A second stouter pull uncovered the face.

" Helen, here ! Here, this minute ! Lord-a-
massy on us ! It 's Jeff Fleming ! "

CHAPTER XII.

IT is needless to describe the emotions of Aunt Helen, or of Nettie, who, after delaying a few minutes at the river, had sensibly come home by herself, rather than wait, or speculate longer on the strange delay of her escort. The emotions of Yankee women do not make them useless; and first of all, they set sharply to work with the aid of the deacon, to take care of their strangely costumed visitor. Amongst them, they hoisted the young man upon a lounge which they set before the kitchen fire, and stripping off his outer garments, and packing him with hot blankets, he soon recovered his senses and told his story.

"We should be very thankful to Almighty God for sparing your life," said the deacon solemnly.

"No doubt," assented Jeff; and, as the deacon turned to say something to Aunt Helen, he added under his breath to Nettie, —

"And for letting me get into danger, too; oughtn't I?"

"Hush!" said Nettie. What else could she say?

6

" I 'm going to get a soft hat," continued Jeff.
" A tall hat is a delusion and a snare."

" Still," remarked Deacon Tarbox, " I have
hitherto found mine safe enough on dry land."

" Deacon," said Jeff, " go a-skating with us next
Saturday afternoon, will you ? "

The Deacon smiled at the young joker ; it was
unnecessary to say any thing.

" Well," observed Jeff after a little, " I believe
I 'm all right, auntie. I 'm sorry to have made
you so much trouble, and slopped up your nice
clean kitchen so."

" Don't say a single word about it," interrupted
the good old lady.

" Well, auntie, I 'll do as much for you some
time, then. I guess I 'll go up street now, at any
rate." And he essayed to rise, but sank back,
looking up at Aunt Helen with a face of such queer
astonishment that she laughed.

" You 'll go straight to bed — that 's what you 'll
do," said she, with decision : " and lie there all day
to-morrow, if necessary, too. Nettie, come and
help me get the south chamber ready."

In truth, the young man's strength seemed to
have dissolved away as if it had melted with the
ice on his clothes. His hands would hardly close
on the back of the lounge, as he tried to help himself to a sitting posture ; he seemed to have no

spine; his legs he could hardly move at all. And as besides he began now to feel intolerably sleepy, he was quite unable to oppose the purpose of his hosts, even if it had been less obviously necessary than it was: So they got out the old-fashioned warming-pan, and inspired with genial warmth the cool depths of the great old-fashioned bed in the guest-chamber; made a nice little fire in the stove; and then deputed the deacon to act as his "grim chamberlain," and see the patient safe under the bed-clothes. Even with the deacon's aid, it was not without a good deal of effort that Jeff crawled upstairs, undressed himself, and got into bed.

Few people know, when they stop at any place, how long they are to stay. Jeff called at Aunt Helen's to get dried and warmed, as the great and good Dr. Isaac Watts went to Sir Thomas Abney's for a visit. He did not, like the famous divine, stay all his life, and at last die in these casual quarters, but he staid all night, and then staid ten weeks; and he came near enough to dying, besides. Before morning he was taken with very sharp pains in his chest, — indeed, he waked up all of a sudden towards daylight with a howl evoked by the first of them, and that evoked besides a couple of extraordinary old ghosts in white to his bedside in a twinkling — to wit, the deacon and Mrs. Tarbox. There was no help for it, however; the old lady, an experienced nurse, said it was — to use her orthoepy — peeripanewmony. She was right in the diagnosis, though obsolescent as to nomenclature. After a pretty tough siege with flannels dipped in hot water, the doctor came, and on examining the patient and hearing the story, looked solemn, prescribed, and, after getting downstairs, questioned Aunt Helen closely about any family tendencies to lung disease. There had been one or two cases, it appeared, within a generation or two. "Then," said the doctor, "we must be all the more careful; that's all. One thing is in his favor, — he has plenty of strength, and, I judge, perfectly clean health. So no need to be frightened at present, though he's a pretty sick man."

You see, the doctor knew Aunt Helen. Doctors will talk pretty plainly to people that they know are safe; none are more close-mouthed, however, to fools.

Well, Jeff had a long fight with the cruel enemy that had seized him. As often happens where people have never been ill, disease seemed to take his physical frame by surprise, and to master it and ravage it before it could organize its defence, like a horde of barbarians swooping down without notice upon a wealthy and peaceful land. When

once, however, the assault was exhausted, though
it left him for the time being a mere phantom of
himself, his recovery was steady and natural.
All the time he was incessantly nursed and petted,
by the deacon and the two women. Their care,
the doctor said, certainly shortened his imprisonment a fortnight; and he jocosely threatened to
collect of them a suitable addition to his fees.
Throughout the first stage of the disease, there
was nothing for them to do except to be strict in
following the doctor's directions, and to wait.
But when the danger and the pain were over, and
the time came when only weakness was left, and
the sick man could begin by tiny gradations to
resume something of the enjoying part of life,
though at first with a passiveness much more complete than that of an infant, then came the empire
of the women. Except the transactions of a
mother over her child, nothing can exceed the
proud authority, and immense sense of fulfilling a
destiny, which a woman displays in tending a
sick person, — more especially if it is a favorite
and a man. Why not? As the stoical stock-
broker observed on hearing the roar of the lions,
" Let 'em roar, for that 's their biz." Nor was the
deacon a whit behindhand, according to his lights.
To be sure, he would have made a very poor fist
at displaying the occasional bouquets of hot-house

flowers with which Nettie used now and then to beautify the room; and as he was one of those opprobriums of the late Lowell Mason, who can't sing, nor learn to sing, any more thán a three-córnered file working across a handsaw, so he would have made wild work with Nettie's ever ready songs. Nor could he compound the magical confections of every kind, wherewith dear old Aunt Helen used to gratify his appetite, that grew more and more ravenous as he gathered strength, the old lady sitting by in the extremest happiness while he demolished in five minutes some delicacy whose harmless and nourishing yet flavorsome quality had occupied her, more or less, very likely, for half a day.

But the deacon could talk, and he could read aloud; and, when Jeff gathered strength enough, he used to take his turn in these employments with the ladies; and the kind old soul was just as happy in it as they were.

" You are three angels, you three," said Jeff one day, as they all stood at his bedside. " I didn't know there were any such people in the world." And the tears stood in his eyes; for when one is so very weak, one cries very easily. However Jeff laughed too, though rather feebly, and finished his extravaganza. " When you three get to heaven, you won't know the difference, for you

can't be a bit better than you are now, and
you won't find you're a bit better thought of.
Angels are plenty there; stay here, where you are
needed."

As for the choice of reading, Nettie brought
mild new novels from the Young Men's Institute
Library. She got pretty much whatever she
wanted from kind-hearted Mr. Boltwood, for the
sake of the sick man, who was one of his con-
stituents, and a favorite, — as he was, in fact, with
everybody who knew him. Aunt Helen used to
listen a while, sometimes, to these wonderful pro-
ductions; but her sound sense and practical piety
were usually unable to bear the unnatural atmosphere very long. She would shake her head, and
rise and depart, saying, that, for her part, she
thought that there must be a special providence
for young folks nowadays, to preserve them
through all the nonsense they read. Her selec-
tions were different; she often chose some book
of travels in the Holy Land or the East; such as
Warren's "Recovery of Jerusalem," which, in
spite of its dry method and confused arrangement,
she read — as it deserves — with close attention
and great delight, from title-page to *finis*. The
story of the wonderful Moabite stone, too, en-
chanted her, Jeff insisted, exactly as "Robinson
Crusoe" or the "Arabian Nights" does a small

boy. So did Rawlinson's " Five Great Monarch-
ies," and any other books she could get hold of,
of the class which may be called unintentional
illustrations of Scripture. And, indeed, they are
the best supports and the best commentaries on
that wonderful book, the unitary and symmetrical
heart-growth and chronicle of sixteen hundred
years of the existence of man, and of God's
words and works through him. The deacon,
again, chose an entirely different department;
and by the way, Jeff showed his natural tact —
unless it was merely the languid passiveness of an
invalid — in allowing his three angels to choose
their own respective fields wherein to expatiate.
The deacon always read him, firstly, the daily
paper, — one New York one and one Hartford
one, — and many a shrewd and dry comment did
he make upon the chronicles of events, and then
upon the use which the editors, those prophets of
the nineteenth century, made of them in the editorial columns. When this was not enough, — to
tell the truth it usually was, — the good old man
used to confer upon Jeff his greatest literary favor.
That is to say, he would read to him his own daily
portion, which he always took in course, of the
" Exposition of the Old and New Testaments,"
by that great and sound divine, the Rev. Matthew
Henry. Of this monumental work, the worthy

deacon possessed a noble copy of the London edition of 1761, in five volumes folio. In this instructive commentary, the deacon was accustomed to read a suitable portion every evening before family prayers, sometimes to himself, and, occasionally, when he lighted upon some striking passage, aloud, for the good of whomsoever it might concern. No wonder the deacon loved it, and had already read it through in course three times, being now well advanced in the fourth; for, as he was accustomed to say with devout thankfulness, it was, under God, due to the weighty reasonings, and powerful applications of that book, that in his youth he had been brought to a realizing sense of his lost state, and ultimately to a trembling hope that he had laid fast hold upon eternal life. It used to put Jeff asleep.

Nothing has thus far been said of two concernments wherewith it might seem that Jeff should have had something to do during this illness of his; namely, his own family, and Jane Burgess. Reason enough: Jeff had no family; and it was this solitary position of his in the world which caused the simple, hearty, genuine, old-fashioned New England kindness of Deacon Tarbox's family to make all the more impression upon him. Both his parents had died long ago; he had indeed been brought up in great measure by some excellent

6*   I

people, who had been friends of his father and mother, and who treated him with helpful kindness, and shrewdly managed his little inheritance. But they were not letter-writing persons; and, in fact, neither were Deacon nor Mrs. Tarbox. The news of Jeff's illness went to Greyford in Nettie's letters to her father, therefore, but as the young man was in the best possible hands, neither letters nor visits were made necessary, and none came. As for Jane Burgess, she was also far less of a letter-writer than Nettie or Rachel. Besides, she was enveloped — as all of us are in this world — in webs of circumstance; things had been happening to her in Boston, for an account of which the reader is referred to the next chapter.

After Jeff Fleming had removed to his own room at the Dove-cot again, had resumed his usual employment at the store, and was rapidly laying hold once more upon all the avocations of his busy life, it was natural that he should still feel far more as if Deacon Tarbox's house was his home, than as if he was a stranger there; so he was at the house even more frequently than before his illness, with or without any excuse.

One pleasant evening, when the Deacon and his wife had gone out to an evening meeting at the South Church, Jeff and Nettie sat chatting alone in the " keeping-room."

"Nettie," said Jeff, "I always used to be afraid of you. I thought you were a sharp-tempered girl, and you certainly used to snap like a pea in a hot skillet sometimes. Have you grown quiet? I don't inquire whether you have grown sweet-tempered, for I have found out that you always were *that.*"

"I think I have grown quiet," said Nettie, blushing. "I love Aunt Helen; and I believe it would make anybody quiet, and good too, to live with her. But I am able to snap, as you call it, on occasion."

"No, please. At least, Nettie, I don't mean to give you any occasion to snap me. I like you ever so much better as you are. It is like finding a sweet heart inside of — no; nobody can fancy you with a rough outside."

"Nor a sweetheart, either," said Nettie, twisting his words.

Jeff answered, this time with something very much like a blush on his part, —

"It would not be right to *fancy* you a sweetheart, Nettie. Nothing less respectful than a strong love and a deep longing should be offered to you; a fancy for you would be an impertinence. You are too good."

"Well, Jeff," replied the young lady, "I don't know why you should say all the pretty things.

Thank you very much for so many compliments;
and you shall have one for yourself.   Aunt Helen
was saying to-day that she never in her life saw a
man before that was perfectly good-natured and
patient in sickness.   So that you are angel number
four, you see."

"Ah, Nettie!" he said, with a good deal of
emotion, "unless you have lived all your life with
strangers, you don't know how such good deeds as
yours and Aunt Helen's make a person good.   I
imagine you people would make Judas Iscariot
into the best creature in the world.   I couldn't
have been cross with you or her by me, any more
than water could freeze in the fire.   It wasn't I
that was sweet-tempered; it was you."

"Aren't you going to allow any thing at all for
uncle?" said Nettie, who, so differently from most
handsome young women, heartily liked to be
praised, and was no more inclined to resent Jeff's
pretty speeches than a house-cat is to resent
stroking.

"Yes, indeed.   Haven't I always reckoned him
one of the angels of this house?   But it's queer
—I can't be near as fond of him as I can of Aunt
Helen and you.   He isn't so pretty.   He isn't so
nice to kiss."

"You don't know, sir.   *I* like to kiss him."

"Well, Nettie, you may kiss him for me, then,
—I wish"—

"What?"

"I mean, won't you give me a little music?"

"Certainly." And she opened the piano and sat down; looking up at him as he took his usual place behind her left shoulder, with a smile that was sunshine itself. "What shall it be?"

"I don't know, Nettie."

"Well, then, take my last piano solo, to begin with."

She played a "Hungarian March." At least, that was the name printed on it, and it was written on the square-built "four-four" basis which is called "march time;" but nevertheless it was a wild, sweet, strange melody too, such as might be imagined to have arisen in the heart of some gypsy musician uttering the nameless yearnings of his mystic Oriental soul, amid the rich influences of sunny vineyards and glorious rivers in the noble land of Hungary.

"O Nettie!" said Jeff; "once more, please." Music which is very beautiful calls upon those who are sensitive to it, with a voice that is almost a sharp pain. It searches the depths of pure emotion, very far below the shallow ripples of criticising judgment or even of conscious observation. Jeff Fleming's voice was unsteady, but the trifling words were full of pleading, — if pleading had been necessary. In truth, the very lovely

music was breaking the ice in another realm than
that of the wintry river ; and Nettie, who felt the
music, perhaps, even more than he, without knowing it, felt that there was more pleading in the
request than merely for a few measures of music.
She shivered slightly, but only answered, —

" Yes, certainly." Could she have had a double
meaning ? Could she have felt — not perceived —
any unspoken wishes from her companion ? And
she played the piece again, the delicate, firm
fingering, the unusually quiet movements of her
shapely smooth fingers upon the keys, adding that
curious magic to the music which depends upon
the appearance of producing much effect with little
motion. This time, neither of them said a word ;
but each knew that the other was greatly moved.

Without speaking, Nettie modulated through a
few soft chords, paused a moment, and played
another piece, belonging in the same chapter of
sentiment with the former, yet sadder. It was so
much more melancholy, in fact, that when the last
soft cadence ended, and Nettie's hands lay motion-
less upon the keys of the final chord, Jeff said, as
if speaking to himself, —

" Why — it is all full of tears."

Nettie, with a little start, turned back the open
leaf, and pointed to the title. " Les Larmes," it
read.

She looked up once more, into Jeff's face, half turning round upon the piano-stool. Jeff could see that her long dark eyelashes were wet.

" Do you feel it so much too ? " he asked.

" Indeed, yes," she said ; and added, with her sunshiny smile, " But if you can tell so well what the music says, what was the other ? "

The witch ! I half believe she knew what she was about. Jeff looked down into her eyes for a moment.

" May I tell you ? "

She could not quite frame to say yes ; she said not a word. Her eyes fell ; but Jeff quickly but lightly passed his arms around her, and kissed her beautiful red lips three times.

" The music said it, Nettie," he said, as she sprang up, but he caught her hand. " I say it for myself, too, Nettie. I love you. Mayn't I ? "

It is of course possible that if the old people had staid at home, and the piano had been kept shut, Nettie and Jeff would not have become engaged to each other, at least not that night. As it was, they did.

CHAPTER XIII.

IT was Jane's first visit with her sister Sophy. Also it was her sister's first winter in Boston.

Ned Bardles had made his fortune in Cottonswick, where he lived over a dozen years. Since then he had been a year in St. Louis; afterwards, he and his wife spent six months in Paris. This was very convenient for Mrs. Bardles, because she could pick up all her furniture there for the house Ned had been building on the new land. For the original Bardleses were Boston people.

Happily it was a large house, for it was one through which the whole Bardles family swept, from morning till night. Aunts, uncles, cousins, sisters, sisters-in-law, and brothers ditto, made it their grand central *rendezvous*. It might be called the Bardles highway. There were walls to the house; but they shut in and never shut out.

Not that Ned Bardles showed a special partiality for his own family, but there were so many of them! And only Jane and her aunt on the Burgess side. It was Ned who had suggested that

Jane should come and spend the winter with them.
Sophy had determined that she would bring his
youngest sister, Christine, into society that very
winter, and she was to be with them for the grand
object of her coming out. Ned had said that he
did not think it was fair to have Christine all that
time, unless Sophy had as long a visit from her
sister. So it was settled they should both be
asked; and in the preparations for receiving them,
if Sophy selected any thing particularly pretty for
the room she was fitting up for Christine, Ned was
sure to find the counterpart of it, — perhaps a
little bit more costly, for Jane's.

Let us explain that Ned Bardles was by no
means what would be called a liberal man. He
had made every cent of his money himself, and
all too carefully, one by one, not to know the value
of every coin of it. But he was just beginning
to enjoy the charm of spending, and finding out
how large his " margin " was. It is not every
millionaire that reaches this bit of knowledge, to
be sure. But, again, he might not have been so
liberal, had Jane been in any way dependent upon
him. Happily the Burgess property had cut up
well between the two daughters. Jane for the
first time began to appreciate this when she came
to stay with her brother-in-law. She had before
felt the comfortable consciousness of owning prop-

erty, — of the family mansion, that could always be a roof for her old age ; but the activity of the Bardles establishment suddenly showed her the outside charm of money, its pleasant chink, and the delight of changing the coin for some equivalent. Jane did not get away from Greyford till the winter was half over, when an old widow friend of her aunt's had turned up to stay some months, with her two daughters, and there was no special reason why Jane should be needed there.

Jane Burgess was one of those receptive beings in whom everybody confides. She was never a confidant, because she was never in the habit of telling her own secrets to another ; but, if such a villanous word could be allowed, she was a faithful *confidee*. She could not sit in a railroad-station two minutes, but what some Irish mother had given her all her history. Indeed, she knew the heart's romance of that stoical creature who keeps the ladies' room of the station. It was also asserted that a horse-car conductor had one day sat down by her side, to tell her about his wife's breaking her leg. She knew the sorrows and joys of everybody in Greyford. Therefore she had not been in her sister's house more than a week, before she had been consulted by every member of the family, about some little intricacy. This was fortunate for Jane, because the first morning after

her arrival, when they were fairly through breakfast, and she stood for a few moments at the
bow-window, looking down the broad street, she
suddenly felt all the loneliness of a new place. A
bit of home-sickness came over her for dear old
Greyford, where she had her set of friends who
really needed her. "Nobody wants me here," she
said to herself.

Sophy, to be sure, was full of occupation, not
merely with her six children in the nursery, and
the six servants who were to oversee them, but
with the successive demands of each day: there
was evidently plenty to do. At the breakfast-
table the plans for the day had been talked over;
and the question was, which of all the proposed
things could be done, and how every thing could
be got into one short day. Sophy had left the
table, saying, " Well, it's no use planning; somebody will be in and change it all. There's only
one thing certain, — we shan't do what we have
settled to do."

Now, this was just what Jane hated. So she
said to herself, as she stood by the window. She
had been in the habit of leading a well-ordered life.
She had her Monday duties, as well as her Sunday
ones; and could sit down Saturday evening, with
her work-basket well cleared out, and a feeling
that the week and its work had been smoothed off

even. What was she going to do in this grand
chaos, where there was no especial orbit marked
out for herself, but, what was worse, those that
had orbits amused themselves by dashing into
those of other people? It ended, as we have seen,
in her becoming the confessor of all. Her reverie
of the first morning had been broken by Christine's
exclamation, —

"Now, Miss Burgess, do give me your opinion!
Shall it be green, or blue? they are equally becoming to me."

Before the end of the week Christine was calling
her "Jeanie," a shortening of her name, and an
endearment, that nobody had ever ventured on
before.

Sophy had confided to her that she hoped Christine would marry a certain Mr. Archer, a second
cousin of the Bardles family, whom she thought
every thing of; and she hoped Jane would do all
she could to assist her.

Ned had introduced another young man to Jane
with especial pomp and ceremony, afterwards
explaining to her that his prospects were admirable, and his family of the best, whom, he had
settled, would just do for Christine.

Meanwhile Christine had confided to Jane her
own little passion, — quite another "party."

Each of Mr. Bardles's three married sisters took

Jane to drive, in their respective *coupés*, on several afternoons, and each gave her the history of their prosperity, and their plans for the rest of the family. His two married brothers, living one on each side of him, told her almost every day what they were worth.

She knew which was the favorite chair of the old-bachelor uncle, and could make the deaf old aunt hear. Aunt Maria, who always had something severe to say to her nephews and nieces, managed to hear whatever she was not expected to; just as it is the near-sighted people who pick up the pins, and see the basting-threads. The little crippled nephew, who was lifted out of the carriage, and laid tenderly on the sofa, to spend the day with Aunt Sophy, learned to look wistfully round for Jane who showed him the pictures so gently and kindly.

All of those who found it so easy to pour their pleasures and their trials into Jane's ear never thought of asking any reciprocal confidences from her. Their pleasure was in recounting and dwelling upon their own triumphs, and trotting themselves out as heroines and heroes before such a ready listener. The invalid boy, indeed, did look anxiously at times to see if Jane were tired of sitting by him, and would hope that he was not keeping her from any thing more pleasant. And

Christine had, at first, wanted to get at the romance of Jane's life; for she was wondering very much whether she was perhaps broken-hearted (how delightfully interesting that would be, if it were so!) at the conduct of Jeffrey Fleming. She had heard they were engaged; and now he was spending the winter in Hartford, and Jane never had any letters from there, she was sure. But she never got any confidences from Jane on the subject. The latter was one of those who not only could keep a secret, but always gave the air of having no secret to keep. And all this was done by merely quietly going on as Jane Burgess, just as she did in Greyford. Only, to Sophy's astonishment, Jane was greatly admired in society. That is a thing nobody can set down any law for; even Mr. Buckle couldn't. Sophy thought it was because Jane took to crimping her hair; perhaps it was so.

CHAPTER XIV.

JANE is by no means the beauty of this story. It has, perhaps, been sufficiently explained that Rachel Holley is. For Rachel always looked like a beauty, wherever you put her. Whether it was her grace, the pose of her classical head, or the glitter of her golden hair, it would be difficult to say. But, however you took her, she had a way of making a frame about herself, and turning into a real picture, whether it was when she stood in the parlor doorway to bid you good-by, or if she were kneeling at Mrs. Worboise's feet to put on that lady's "Arctics," to go to an evening meeting.

But Jane was always composed, equal to the occasion, and had the grand fund of reserve on hand that always is impressive.

There was one person who laid a special claim to Jane's sympathy, and it was acknowledged by all the Bardles family. This was Mark Hinsdale. He had been received there kindly, and soon became one of the many expected guests who were allowed to drop in at any time. There was a seat for him at the dinner-table, plans for him for the evening's concert, theatre, or party, whatever it might be.

Of course, Mark also had to consult and confide with Jane. Every new plan which took form, as he sat in the library waiting of a rainy day for anybody to come and ask for a "sermon-book," or for "another book," would be dashed down on paper, to be sent to her. With his vivid imagination, these plans instantly assumed their full proportions; and, as he wrote, the detail wrought itself out, even to refinement. This would all be posted to Jane, and the next time Mark called he would expect her judgment on the whole. It was sometimes a play, sometimes a novel; always it was to be very successful when it had found a publisher, and always Jane was expected, from having read the brief, to retain a complete knowledge of each character, and of all the names. Here, for instance, is the plan of "Bertie Gwynne."

LIBRARY, Monday Morning.

DEAR JANE, — I have had a most interesting talk with an army officer, who has been for three years surveying on the Plains. He has shot buffalo, and, I dare say, scalped Indians, and knows every thing. He knows all our eastern wilderness just as well. What he says confirms my plan for "Bertie Gwynne." Just look at this table of contents.

The detail of the book is so extensive, that I cannot give you the plot, but you can read this.

BERTIE GWYNNE.

Book 1. ON BOARD THE SERINGA.

1. Waiting.
2. The Captain's Story.
3. Ended and Begun.
4. Mamelita.
5. In the Mexican Inn.
6. Captain Hathaway in Command.
7. The Wreck of the Seringa.

Book 2. SOUTH-WEST AND NORTH-WEST.

1. In the Indian Country.
2. The Old Patriarch.
3. Escape.
4. Norah Burke's Suitor.
5. The Signing of the Deed.
6. Father and Son.
7. Charley Phinney's Departure.

Book 3. LITTLE CAPTAIN.

1. History of the Bucker Family.
2. Little Captain's Education.
3. Eden in New England.
4. The Mail comes in.
5. The Mail goes out.

Book 4. SILVERSPURS.

1. The Phinney Corporations.
2. Conchita and Panchita.
3. An Unexpected Arrival.

4. The Ball and its Results.
5. Silverspurs to the Rescue!
6. Through the Desert.
7. The Waterspout.
8. The Story of Silverspurs.
9. News from Home.

Book 5. RISEN FROM THE DEAD.

1. The New Home.
2. In the Old Churchyard.
3. Rest.

I think that if I am ever to do any thing good, it will be in this story, which will attempt to trace the growth of a soul with only Nature to come in contact with it; which will be full of the life and adventure of sea and land, of North Atlantic and South Pacific shores; which will be exciting, yet in no way offensively sensational.

This is the story I told you of at the theatre, — a story which you declared was certainly not immoral, though it might not be moral. It has grown to artistic completion, and unfolded now something like a moral, — a relation of heroic self-sacrifice.

In just the same freedom, Mark would have his budget of sorrows to bring to Jane. Over and over again he talked with her about Rachel Holley.

" It is something I can't stand, to think of Rachel spending the winter in a second, no, fifteenth-rate boarding-house in New York, when we might just as well have been married, and be living comfortably here in Boston."

Now, Jane knew that Mr. Holley had nothing in particular to give his daughter if she should be married; and she, privately, did not exactly see how Rachel and Mark were going to live so very comfortably on his little salary as assistant librarian; especially as Mark, when he said these words, would look round approvingly upon all the Bardles luxury about them, as though he and Rachel had only to step into just such a home.

Mark was an unpractical being; he had lived in his books all his life. His gleam of Rachel was all that had ever waked him out of his dreamy reading. As he sat in a comfortable chair in the Bardles back parlor, he thought how delightful it would be to be living with Rachel in a home of his own, much like this, only he should turn the back parlor into a library; and — and — it was very agreeable to explain it all to the listening Jane.

Jane defended Rachel, and gradually brought Mark to acknowledge that perhaps she was right in not being in such a hurry to be married. Then, afterwards, he came to be glad that Rachel was in New York, on Horace's account; for the poor fellow must be sadly cut up at Nettie's treatment of him. Indeed, Mark in a short time began to be consoled, and the stir and bustle of the Bardles family interested him, and woke him up from his

dreamy life.   He brought them all the new books:
these they could look at, if they had not time for
more, and it was very convenient to have him to
tell what there was in the books, when they didn't
read them.

It must not be supposed, that, for all these con-
fessions, Jane had any private chapel or oratory
set apart; there was no privacy in the Bardles
family.   The two drawing-rooms opened upon
each other with wide folding doors.   In the back
room, Jane and Christine took their French lessons
three mornings in the week.   But aunts and
uncles poured in upon the lesson all the same.
The sisters liked the chance to come in and talk
a little French with M. Pinaud.   Aunt Maria,
of course, always happened in, just as they were
looking for a little quiet, and always it was necessary to explain to her what was going on.

"Oh, a French lesson! I hate the French,"
was the regular answer, which it was hoped
M. Pinaud would not understand, though it
was given in so loud a voice he could not but
hear.

Just in the height of the *mêlée*, the six children
would come down, on their way out for their noon
walk; and the stairway opening between the
rooms, it gave an admirable chance to stop them,
and have a great time with them.   Retty's new

suit had to be admired, and Johnny's leggings,
and Carl's new hobby-horse, that his father
brought from New York; and they each had a
favorite aunt, who pounced upon her especial pet;
and all the children had to learn to say "*Bon
jour*" to M. Pinaud. The little infantry procession swept off, at last; some of the aunts with it.
But, by this time, there was luncheon, and everybody had to go down to that; and afterwards
came callers, or calls to be made till dinner, and
in the evening a rush always. When there was
no French lesson, there was shopping. For afternoons, again, there were the *matinées*, afternoon
concerts, or drives.

Yet in such a rush, the moments stolen for confidence are only the more sweet. If one has the
whole day for conversation, it gets a little diluted
and weak. But, if you must concentrate all you
want to say into the favored moment, you naturally make it concise, and to the point. That is,
a long cultivation teaches you to do so. Often,
after all, you bring out only the most unnecessary
and vapid part of what you have to say, just as so
many people take up half their letters in explaining how they have not written before, a fact already painfully evident.

"Jeanie, you must sit by me to-night at the
play," Christine would whisper to Jane. "I have

got such a story to tell you!" And the moment of confidence had to be fought for; it never came of itself.

One day, when noon at the Bardles house was especially uproarious, Mark came to Jane's side to try to say something to her. The children were all on their way out for their walk. Johnny was shrieking with delight on the back of the bachelor uncle, who was trotting him up and down the length of the two rooms. Sophy was telling the price of the feather in Retty's hat to two of her sisters-in-law, on the opposite side of the room, to whom she had to scream out the valuable information. Aunt Maria was explaining to the company in general her views upon the French war. She thought the Communists had better have been left to kill each other, and then, when there was not a Frenchman to be seen, the English could take Paris: which she wondered they didn't do, after Waterloo.

M. Pinaud was just taking his leave, and Christine was attempting to drown her Aunt Maria's voice in a flood of French; but she was not very ready in that language, and ended by going off in a list of the numerals, which she could say easily. It did not make much difference what she said, in the hubbub; and the French teacher was only too glad to get off, without crushing Sallie's wax doll that lay in the stairway.

"I should like to walk with you to the opera, Jane, to-night. I have something to tell you," was all Mark found a chance to say.

/

CHAPTER XV.

WHEN evening came, there was some talk of
Jane's going in the carriage with old Mrs.
Bardles; but she stoutly resisted, and was allowed
to set off, taking Mark's arm. A boy, one of Ñed
Bardles's younger brothers, hitched on to them for
part of the way, but happily found their conversation dull, and they had a few moments to each
other. The information Mark wanted to give
Jane was something he had learned of Jeffrey
Fleming. That constant young man had never
written to Jane any thing about his long illness.
Nor had Nettie written to tell her of it. Jane
had heard not a word from him for many weeks.
Some one had told Mark that Jeffrey had been
dangerously ill, and Mark directly wrote to Hartford to inquire about it. A letter came from Jeffrey himself, to say that it was all true; but he
was well again, and now "dead in love with
Nettie," as he expressed it.

Jeffrey had always been a wild young fellow,
never capable of sticking to one thing long.

There had only been one bit of steadfastness in him, and that was his affection for Jane. There had always been something in her serene atmosphere, that had brought out all his finer qualities, — so everybody thought. And it was considered one of Jane's saintly gifts, that of loving such a harum-scarum, and bringing him into respectable society.

How could Mark impart to Jane the intelligence of Jeffrey's shameful desertion?

It was Jane who helped him out. She, too, had a piece of intelligence for him. She had received a letter from Rachel, telling about her life in New York, and how much she was depending upon Horace Vanzandt's tenderness and affection.

"I do believe, if he ever loved Nettie," said Rachel, "he loves her no longer. And certainly she is not worthy the love of one so whole-souled as he is, if she could treat him as she has done!"

Jane thought she ought to prepare Mark for the fact that Rachel was finding some consolation in Horace in his absence; and, knowing that her time was short, she plunged directly into it. This made it amazingly easy for Mark to tell his part; and he was so eager in abusing Jeffrey Fleming, that he forgot to be as sorry as he ought about Rachel.

It was with Mark's intelligence ringing in her ears that Jane sat through the opera.

7*

The action of an opera is often supposed to be unnatural and absurd; but the writer of the *libretto* knows well the power of the music that is to lift the whole story into a reality. And, if one listens to the opera with any great emotion on one's mind, it is astonishing how its music allies itself to one's feelings and makes the stage carry out the drama that is going on in the heart.

We almost believe that music is a necessary accompaniment to all the tragedy or action of our own lives; and when the orchestra stops, and the curtain falls, we come out into the silence, or into the hubbub that follows the harmony, with the feeling that our little play is ended too, and that there is nothing more.

Even when a grinding organ is playing at the corner of the streets, look round and you will see how unconsciously everybody's pace is set in time with the melody, — old men, and little girls, and busy shopping-women, — and some of them go moving on with an earnest, heroic look, as though the music of the spheres were suddenly sounding up through the discordant noise of the street.

The drama of Jane's life was coursing through her mind, all the time she was listening to the three acts of the opera. Between the parts, Christine on one side would bring in a little chippering about somebody's bonnet; but on the other side

Mark was sitting silent, having fallen back into one of his moods.

The opera was "Il Trovatore." Jane was going over some of her old times with Jeffrey, one evening, when she had saved him from a terrible temptation, when he had staid by her, and gave her all the history of his life, telling her scenes that had been then a black contrast to her own peaceful life, that had made her shudder, and were recalled again in the clangor of the chorus on the stage, by the great tumult of the orchestra.

Again the scene changed, and she thought of him on his sick-bed, and perhaps wanting her again. She had discouraged Jeffrey's writing to her, partly because he wrote such poor letters, and partly because, as she told him, he ought to be devoting himself to his business; and, if he were writing every day to her, it would take out a great piece of his time. And she did not think much of now-and-then letters, when one has every thing to tell, and tells nothing. Besides, Jane had a difficulty in trusting her own thoughts even to paper. . It frightened her, the very idea of seeing her own heart laid down in black and white before her eyes. For this reason Jane had always written very cold, unsatisfactory letters.

And now on the stage there was the scene of a high tower at one side. Behind it was the tenor, singing with all his might off the stage, supposed to be in the uppermost story of the tower.

What a voice he had! How rich, how tender, how moving! He was reproaching the lady of his love for leaving him, for deserting him to marry another. But there she was below, singing with all her voice, out of her heart, too, trying to reach way up to him from the foot of the tower, telling him how she loved him, and how she wanted to come to him, and to save his life. And all the time from the distance came the *Miserere*, the chanting of some quiet nuns singing in this heavenly way out of the peace of their cells, and sending their harmony into the discords of the world. It was a chorus with many monotones, however: what sympathy did it have with two hearts storming and breaking outside?

Well, all this, to Jane, became her own drama.

And have we not all of us acted and lived it through in all our lives? We call the plot of the opera absurd and unnatural and ridiculous. Oh, yes! so it all is, — the bridegroom with his white satin breeches, loose at the knee, lace-trimmed; the stout basso, brawling his woes. But have we not seen the being we loved the most, imprisoned in some tower, and we at the foot of it, outside, grasping the cold stones, trying to reach to him? It is sickness, sin, of ours or his, some impenetra-

- bility, that shuts him from us. We hear his appealing voice, but we cannot come to him; and not far away there is going on the sound of the voices of the peaceful, of those who are feeling no longer the passions of the world, and they chant of death and heaven and pity. But it cannot quiet us; for it is not only our own sorrow, but the agony of another, that is calling to us; and we try to make the voice of our heart reach him with our sympathy, though it must be in discord with the chant. Jane seemed to see Jeffrey on his sick-bed, stretching out his arms to her, appealing to her.

"*Non ti scordar di me*," sang out the opera-singer.

"What, I, separate my heart from yours!" said Jane's thoughts.

"Could not I go to you?"

And then came another pause between the parts of the opera, and everybody fell to saying a few things. Sophy had tears in her eyes, but she only took out her handkerchief to show its embroidery to her neighbor.

Now, in all this, Jane had been thinking not merely of Jeffrey's severe illness, and that she had not been there to care for him; but the sting had been, that another woman had filled what was her province. Jane loved Nettie, as all these three girls loved each other. But Jane had been Jeffrey's strong friend and supporter. There had been periods in his life when she had saved him from himself. She felt, then, a certain right to be every thing to him, — a jealousy of the influence of another.

And Nettie she could not believe was the right woman for Jeffrey; they were too much alike, both fascinating from their very waywardness. Mark had somehow let out in his story that Nettie had changed, had improved.

But who wanted Nettie to improve, or change? Was not she very well as she was? What prosaic, Yankee-calculating kind of books are those that are so stern on the butterflies! Would we indeed prefer them all to stay as caterpillars, and be grubbing round all the time over the foliage? And if the butterfly finds his food in every flower-cup, why need he build little larders, like ants and bees?

Jane did not say all this. The Gypsy was singing her sleepy song, and Jane only felt that it was all wrong, and that it was her fault. If she had not been so stiff about Jeffrey's writing, it would have been different. She would have known of his illness, from his not writing; she would have gone to him.

Christine arranged that Mr. Archer should walk home with Jane, and Mark with herself; so Jane had no more talk with him that night.

CHAPTER XVI.

AFTERWARDS there came fresh opportunities of Jane's having conversation with Mark alone.

Her charitable feelings had been much exercised since she had been in Boston. She could not resist giving an answer to the appeals of " only one cent " from the forlorn boys and girls on Beacon Street. In the first days of her visit, Ned had caught her listening to the story of a ragged woman on the door-steps. He had then lectured her on the subject of the utter uselessness, nay, wickedness, of giving money in such cases ; and he presented Jane with a packet of tickets of the Provident Association, and its little directory of names to whom to apply. Jane made liberal use of these.

But sometimes she could not resist answering such an appeal herself; and she had accumulated a little set of poor places to be visited, that she attended to as carefully as to any of her list of callers. But these places were far away in the narrow, perplexing, winding streets, and she needed Mark as guide. Two or three times a week, then, they set off together on these journeys of discovery.

Such an expedition was not particularly favorable to talking. All the first part of the way they were interrupted by meeting acquaintances; then they reached the streets, where the sidewalks were very narrow, — there was building going on, here and there, and Mark had to shoot off in one direction, and Jane in another. But Mark had a happy faculty of not being disturbed by these outside interruptions, and would hold on to his sentence and his idea, all through the intricacies of street-crossings, crowds and jostlings.

In one of their wanderings, one day, far down at the "North End," they stumbled upon what looked like a bee-hive, or what Mark called a human ant-heap. For little ants of children were running in and out of a little shop from which each came with a ginger-cake in its mouth.

"Suppose we try our chance," said Mark to Jane; "for our long walk makes me feel as if I should like a ginger-cake."

Jane agreed; and they went into a little low shop, the lower story of a house that formed one of a most uninteresting looking block of houses.

But when they were inside, they found it was

the establishment of Luclarion Grapp, of which
Jane had heard. This remarkable woman had set
up a little shop in the most hopeless and poorest
part of the town, for the very purpose of doing
something for the forlorn children that seemed to
swarm about there. She had succeeded, from
washing the face of one child, in purifying the
families of many; and she gladly showed Jane and
Mark up and down through the rooms of her little
home.

"That's a good beginning," said Mark, after
they had left.

"It shows what one woman can do," said Jane.

"Then how much two people could do," said
Mark, "if they set themselves together! But,
Jane, do you know the sight of all such destitution
as we have been seeing here stirs up all my theo-
ries? I begin to wonder what right we have to
any property at all, when these have barely their
daily bread. Not that I am largely endowed with
worldly goods; but I take my little luxuries, and I
am, in my way, working for an independence, for a
competency, that I have hoped to reach some
time.".

Jane was plunging across the street in front of
an omnibus, and her answer was lost.

"Now, I have half a mind," said Mark, "to
start a new order of mendicant friars, throw what

K

little goods I have into the general fund, and set
out begging my daily bread."

"If you came across brother Bardles," said Jane,
for now they had happened to reach a broad sidewalk, and firm footing, where she could talk more
freely, "he would give you a ticket to the Provident Association."

"That's the trouble nowadays," said Mark;
"one is always coming flat up against an institution. If it were only like the old days, when there
was a wide porch to the houses of the great, where
the poor could find their rest, and be sure that
a loaf of bread would be brought to them " —

"But stop a minute, Mark," said Jane; "somebody must then be rich enough to build up your
castle and its wide porch, and somebody has got to
earn and make your bread. Now, I should be a
little ashamed to go round and beg for bread I had
not earned. But perhaps you mean to preach so
grandly that you will be worthy of it."

"Oh, no!" said Mark, in a discouraged tone.
"I am no preacher; but seriously, Jane, is it the
highest life among the rich, or among the poor?
or, rather, won't you tell me what do you think
living — what do you think life is?"

They had reached a crowded place, where all
the horse-cars and all the omnibuses seemed to
have met in one grand jumble, with news-boys,

apple-women, men selling boot-lacings, men with valises, women with huge travelling-bags, all flung together in a grand pell-mell. It was a muddy day, and sidewalks and street were imbedded in a black paste.· Jane had been grasping her dress, and dropping her sunshade every three steps. She succeeded in answering —

" I think it is a little mixed now."

" I agree with you," said Mark, laughing: " it is for us two to pick our course through it, together, cleanly, if we can. What do you say to taking this blue-green horse-car? "

Jane gladly flung herself into it; and Mark, seating himself by her side, went on with his speculations. These were somewhat interrupted, for here they had reached the meridian of acquaintances who were to be greeted in the car. Still Mark held manfully to his thread.

When Jane had a little time to consider it all by herself, she began to tremble a little at her responsibilities with Mark. He was depending upon her, she feared, too much.

In the old days she used to think that the kaleidoscope of fate ought to have jostled Mark and Nettie side by side. Nettie was precisely the gay, lively companion that he needed to stir him from his dreams, and keep him active in life. Now the kaleidoscope had turned, and there was a fresh crystallization in their little circle. Was this to be the permanent one? She began to think so. There was one thing she possessed, that she would gladly give Mark; and that was her fortune. Yes, how pleasant it would be to make for him a comfortable home, with its luxurious library, and to have every thing easy and happy for him. She could do it; and in return he was just the person to make home-life charming, always even in temper, with a steady flow of happy thought and originality that made talk with him delightful. She knew that Mark thought so little of her fortune, that the fact that he was poor and she rich would not stand in the way of his marrying her, because it would not occur to him. He would marry her for love, so conscious of her own worth that he would forget in his unworldliness that she had also the commonplace charms of money. This simplicity touched Jane; and she felt that she would like to keep him in this dream all his life. There were so many about her, who looked at her only as an heiress, that it was refreshing to know how utterly Mark was unconscious of it.

She was a little startled one day, when Mark came in suddenly, and begged to speak with her. She drew back from the accustomed throng in the parlors, into a little anteroom that separated them from the billiard-room in the wing. This was so called because there was a billiard-table there, where all the members of the family were fond of playing. But it communicated by some stairs with the lower story, and Sophy was apt to be holding her domestic household councils here with her servants. So it was by no means a secluded room, and the little anteroom that led to it was quite a thoroughfare.

It was pretty much filled up, too, by a large Daphne plant in flower, and a marble head of Psyche on a pedestal. Mark and Jane managed to stand there a few minutes.

"Jane, I have come to tell you," said Mark, "that I have just received an appointment as head librarian to the Johnsonian Library in Chicago, with a real substantial salary; only I must go there directly."

Sophy rushed through from the billiard-room.

"Where is Ned? Has he got out? I must speak to him."

"To Chicago!" said Jane, when she had answered Sophy: "how singular! For I was going to tell you of our new plans. Ned's brother wants him to come out to Chicago, for this next winter, to oversee some business; and Sophy and I, all of us, are to go next fall. At least, it is settled I am to go if I like. Ned was talking it over this morning at breakfast; and I, indeed, thought I would consult you on my going."

Jane's long sentence had only been brought out with interruptions. Carl, the oldest boy, had dashed through to the billiard-room to find his mother, and back again, not successful in his search. Retty had appeared looking for Cecil. The nurse came rushing after Retty. Cecil had made his way downstairs, but Retty was not to be allowed to follow him; the nurse brought Retty back triumphantly in her arms, screaming at the top of his lungs. He had to be cosseted by his aunt, and then his mother reappeared on the scene to see what was the matter. Then she wanted to consult Jane about making Mr. Jack Bardles stay to dinner, but she flew off again at a scream from Cecil. Aunt Maria was shouting from the front room, wondering where Jane was.

"Of course, of course," said Mark, when he had a chance to speak, "you will come to Chicago. Only let me get there first and establish myself, and then may I write and ask you " —

Christine here plunged in.

"O Jane, Jane! save me from that detestable Mr. Archer. He is coming up the stairs. Do let me have a cosey little chat with you and Mark " —

Mark suppressed some strong language, unusual

to him, and left. He came in the evening to say
good-by, but had only an opportunity of promising to write to Jane.

The next day was Valentine's Day, and this
little poem came to Jane. It was not in Mark's
writing. But could any one except him have
written it?

DAY AND NIGHT.

I.

Though my heart throbs not when I hear her voice,
 Nor moves with every rustle of her dress,
 Still do I know her wondrous loveliness,
And in her rare, sweet beauty I rejoice.
The symbol of all lovely things to me;
 A touch of heaven seems to light her face.
 She is a creature of such perfect grace,
And more than that, such perfect purity,
The world seems better for her living in it.
 To love her, then, can any of us dare?
Her heart a treasure is, — I would not win it.
 It is enough, our breathing the same air.
I know, through her, my life is filled with light.
This is the placid day: oh! must there come a night?

II.

To her alone I can myself disclose;
 She always understands and comforts me.
 So brave, so frank, so generous is she,
So true a friend, that I forget my foes.
So beautiful, with soft yet brilliant eyes,
 And tangled dark brown hair, and youth's rich bloom,
 Where'er she moves is warmth and sweet perfume.
And yet, o'er all this good, such ill may rise:

Though by the future only 'twill be proved,
Too well I know what coming years may bring,
  If, ever loving, she should not be loved.
She will reach ruin through that suffering.
  But now she is all love and life and light.
  It is the joyous day: I will not think of night.

Feb. 14, 1871.

CHAPTER XVII.

VALENTINE'S DAY came in Lent last year, and soon after Easter the Bardles establishment was broken up for the summer wanderings. Jane went for a few weeks to Greyford, but was to spend the summer with her sister Sophy in Newport.

She found that she had just missed seeing Rachel Holley and Horace, in Greyford. Mr. Holley had taken Rachel away with him "out west."

"Somehow, since his wife is dead," said Miss Burgess, Jane's aunt, "Mr. Holley can't seem to settle down to any thing at home. He has gone out prospecting a little. He did talk about Denver City and St. Paul's; but I shouldn't wonder if he settled down before he got there. Mrs. Holley's relations are all in Chicago, and Mrs. Worboise has moved out there, I suppose you heard."

Jane heard, too, that Dr. Sylva and Nettie joined the Holleys, just for the journey, and nobody knew when Nettie would be back.

How quiet Greyford seemed! Jane looked up and down its broad streets, with their huge elms

8

shading it on either side ; and, in the late afternoon, she seemed to see the same cows wandering home that she used to watch when she was a child. They ran wildly into Deacon Spinley's side yard, just as they used to, and were chased out with the same contumely, as it seemed, by the same boy.

One day, while she was with her aunt, she opened a little cupboard that was set into the side of the old-fashioned chimney of the sitting-room, to put away into it some of the things she was tired of seeing on the mantle-piece. She was surprised to find standing in front of one of the shelves, looking at her, a little bear of carved wood, which she had never seen before. She took it out to look at it, when Miss Burgess exclaimed, " There, Jane, I almost forgot to give it to you. Horace Vanzandt left it for you, to show you he had improved in carving since the old days. He put it up on the mantle-shelf; but seeing it was getting dusty, I set it away in the cupboard, and clean forgot it."

It was in very old, childish days that the Vanzandts lived next door to the Burgesses. Horace had a special gift at whittling, and used to make dolls' chairs and tables for Jane, that she kept in her baby-house as long as they would stand. The little Jane valued them, though the legs were rickety; and they were the pride of her establishment.

One day when Horace was about six years old, he was found crying on the door-step. Tears were unusual with this ambitious youth. Jane tried to find out the trouble. He held up a bit of wood in his hand, saying, " I tried to make it a bear, and it will be a pig."

This was a tragic event in childhood, but had been the source of an infinite number of jokes afterwards; Horace insisting that his bears, in after life, turned out nothing but pigs.

" He wants to show me that he can make a bear," said Jane, as she took it upstairs with her. This was on one of her last days of packing, and she did the bear up in tissue-paper, and put it in one of the sacredest trays of her trunk. She had a letter from Mark in the afternoon ; and when she went back to her room she unpacked all her things, took the bear out, and set it up on the mantlepiece.

" I may as well leave it with the rest of my things," she said.

The next morning she went away. She looked round her room before she left, with her travelling-bag in her hand. The little bear sat up on his hind legs, and looked at her. She saw the little bear, took it, and plunged it into the top of her bag.

Sophy went upstairs with Jane to her room,

after she reached Newport, and was present when Jane opened her bag, to take out some of her things. "What a dear little bear!" exclaimed Sophy, when it appeared. "It is just the thing to set on the top of your little clock. I had a plan for a cuckoo-clock for your room, but Ned thought you would not like the noise. And perhaps it is best not to have two in the house. And he found this pretty little carved thing for the mantle-piece. And just what it needs is this little bear."

Jane's summer passed on quietly. Its peace almost terrified her. It made her think of one of those cloudless summer days that are called "weather breeders," and she had a vague dread of a storm collecting behind the horizon.

She had the most charming letters from Mark, full of tenderness and eloquence and poetry. She liked to read them over and over. After she had been especially moved by one of these letters, she would take away Horace's little bear from the top of the clock, and set it aside. But Ann, the housemaid, had an unwonted eye for symmetry, and always found it out and put it back again.

"Of course it's absurd," said Jane to herself, "to make any thing out of such a little thing. But I wonder if Horace meant any thing more than fun, and to show me that he had improved in carving. Yet it keeps me thinking of him; and I can't

see the right of it, that all Mark's letters should
not keep him in my mind so much as the sight of
that little thing makes Horace always present
to me!" ·

As for Mark, he liked Chicago. It would be
hard to find a wide-awake young man, whether he
were poet like Mark, inventor like Horace, or a general, driving, enthusiastic putter-of-things-through
like Jeff, who did not like Chicago in those days,
at least, till he had seen the folly of it. · In the
first place, Chicago was, as Mark's old friend, Dr.
Sylva, was used to say, a central ganglion of the
world's nervous-system, — the life of the world
found its centres there; and then Humfry, on the
other side the table, would laugh, and say, " He
means it is a relay station on the wires," which was
substantially what the Doctor did mean. Everybody was in a hurry; everybody looked forward, and
was so perfectly sure of his future that he dis-
counted it at whatever rate of interest. Mark did
not find that a great many people came into the
Johnsonian Library; but that was all the better
for the librarian. It gave him more time to write
for " The Lakeside Monthly," in which he was an
accepted and favorite contributor. As he walked
home at night, he would stop and see Mr. Walsh,
and look over the last new books, and in his beautiful book-store, that most luxurious of " loafing-

places," turn over some of the new English newspapers. Then, ignoring the horse-cars, he would cross the bridge westward, often stopping to study character or race, as the fresh-water seamen worked their boats or schooners through the drawbridges or up and down the crowded stream. Mark lived in nice rooms with some old friends who kept house well out on the prairie, as he used to say, on the west side. But he did not dislike his walk, night or morning. In the warmest August evenings he came home well contented with himself, and declaring, that if you did not walk fast, the air was not oppressive. This meant, being interpreted, that as he walked he had been blocking out a new novel, or whipping into shape the refractory rhymes of a new sonnet to Jane. To think that that quiet girl, so well-balanced, so little demonstrative, should have got this empire over our bright, intense poet, who cannot sleep to-night unless to paper he has confided what he thinks and what he knows! Ah, Jane! Jane! as he makes "lowly" do its duty in rhyming with "holy," and reserves fit place lower down in which the line is to round off into "melan*choly*," are you reading his last sonnet? or are you looking at Horace's bear?

CHAPTER XVIII.

999 West 12th Street, Aug. 11, 1870.

M<small>Y</small> DEAR MARK, — The Greyford people tell me you are in Chicago. And to think that your old dream is fulfilled, and that you are librarian-in-chief! Shall I not make you order full sets of " Annales des Mines," and " Royal Engineer Transactions," and every thing else in my line? You know, old fellow, that I am to spend next winter in Chicago, and, if things turn out well, all my life. It is one of those hits which fellows here call " *bonus ictus,*" that being supposed to be the Latin for " a good lick."

Do you know any thing about cut-offs? Very likely you do not ; but on the proper management and adjustment of cut-offs depends the very price of the coal that you will burn next winter to warm your Alexandrian library, or whatever its name may be. It is estimated that the truly successful cut-offs now in use diminish the quantity of fuel needed in the steam-engines which employ them by twenty-three, twenty-seven, and in some cases

thirty-five, and even thirty-six and two-thirds per
cent. So you see a cut-off, if it is really good, is
a virtual addition of such an amount as those
figures represent to the coal-product of the country.

Well, we have stumbled on an old fellow —
queer fellow too ; regular down-east Yankee —who
has a most amazing and ingenious invention for a
new cut-off. If you were here I could explain it
to you in two minutes; but without a working
model you would hardly understand it. I have
just sent off to London, where we are to get an
English patent, some capital drawings of it by
Rachel, which would make you understand it perfectly. No matter. Some friends of mine have
an interest in the patent for the whole North-west,
with the exception of Davenport, Dubuque, and
two or three other cities, which had been sold
before. We propose to establish one good shop to
begin with, as our head-centre ; and the question
now is where it shall be put. I have been rather
in favor of Chicago myself, it is such an advantage
to be at a central point. Wherever it is established, Chicago will be my central point for some
months, till we are ready to begin, for I have the
oversight of all the sub-contracts we make.

Oddly enough, as very likely you know, our old
friend, Mrs. Worboise, at whose adventures you

have heard us laugh so much, is established there. Would you mind going round to see her, and finding out surreptitiously whether I can go to her direct when I come? If I write and ask, she will turn out the best inmates she has; Abe Lincoln and his wife and Thad would have to go to make room for me, if she could not provide otherwise. But if you think she has a decent attic, or other landing-place, which I can have without ruining her, just engage it for me, and let me know. They tell me business was never opening so briskly in Chicago. But I believe that is what you Western fellows always say. How soon I shall be saying "we Western fellows!" It will be real good to live in the same "school deestrict" with you again, old fellow. Good-by.

Yours for ever,
HORACE VANZANDT.

Mark was thoroughly glad to find that one of the old set was coming out to be near him, though it were but for a time. Of course, he found that Mrs. Worboise had room enough for Horace, and he was only sorry that he had established himself on the West Side. She was in that part of the city well at the southward, where it begins to become a little open, and her good spacious house had room enough and to spare for Horace and his

8*   L

belongings. Well pleased was she to know that
fate had thrown him under her roof again. Mark
was quite sure that the letter gave him pleasure
so far. He was also sure that it gave him no pain
— no, no sort of pain — to find Horace speaking
of Rachel and Rachel's drawing as if he were so in
the habit of regarding her as entirely his own
property, that there need be no explanation why
she was drawing illustrations of specifications for
him. He was sure this gave him no pain. But
he wondered a little why it gave him no pain.
He knew very well, that ever since Valentine's
Day, and before, every poem he had written to
anybody had been written to Jane Burgess.
There was a true woman, who could appreciate
him and his. Still, he could not but remember,
also, that night when Rachel's mother died, and
the verses he wrote to her the next Valentine's
Day ; and, indeed, he remembered that he wished
he knew how he could ask her for a little drama
of his, called " The Pearl in the Well," which he
had sent to her with a pretty dedication, and
which nobody had any copy of excepting her.
He was not quite sure but he could get it brought
out at Crosby's Opera House ; and, if he had not
wholly dropped correspondence with Rachel, he
would write and ask her for it. It puzzled him
a little to know, first, how he ever could have

thought that she was so good a critic of his work; and, second, why he was not more jealous of Horace, of whom, in fact, he was not jealous at all.

Of which mysteries the explanation was simple enough to anybody who could look at them without the obscuring films which clouded Master Mark's vision. He and Rachel Holley had been to school together, and had gone home together. She had ridden on his sled, and, in return, had taught him to play cat's-cradle. Then she had become a woman at the period when he was ceasing to be a boy, but had not become a man. Being the woman he knew best, he honored her, prized her, and supposed he loved her. It is a mistake which often happens where propinquity, as Miss Edgeworth calls it, has brought a boy and girl together. The woman Rachel judged the situation better than the fledgling Mark; and this was the reason why Rachel did not engage herself to him, when he plead so earnestly, and wrote verses which were so pretty, after her mother's death.

But Mark was to become a man in his time. A dreamy man, if you please; a man who did not yet know much about how the wolf was to be kept from the door, or whether the little god of love could or could not turn the spit. Still, he was a man. Being a man, he had been thrown into near and confidential intercourse with another charming woman, Jane Burgess. Who, indeed, was not in confidential intercourse with this sympathetic Jane? Yet, again, she was the first cultivated and accomplished woman whom the man Mark Hinsdale had seen nearly. Being the woman he knew best, he honored her in turn, prized her, and supposed he loved her. He wrote her very pretty. verses, and sent her very charming letters. He certainly loved her as he had never loved Rachel, and that was really the reason why he was not in the least jealous of Horace Vanzandt. But all this, which it is easy enough for all of us to understand, was not so clear to Mark, who could not understand that as lately as two years ago he was in that transition condition of the polliwog, or the tadpole, which, by the more careful writers in anthropology, is called the condition of the hobbledehoy.

CHAPTER XIX.

THE Bardles family, with full contingents of nurses for the children, even with a man-servant who was to see to the baggage, as if it needed any seeing to, and with Jane, of course, had gone to sleep at Rochester, N. Y., and had waked some forty miles east of Windsor, opposite Detroit, in Canada. Jane had gulped down an immense regret when she had found that she was to be trundled by Niagara, actually "in full sight of the cataract," as Ned Bardles told her, without any idea of the pain he gave her, and that she was not to have any sight of it, not even to be waked to see the shimmer of the white spray in the moon-light, nor to hear the roar of the water. She even had rebellious plans that she would sit up till mid-night and go out upon the platform as they passed, if so she might fulfil the dream of twenty years, and at least feel that she had "seen Niagara." But no one gave the least countenance to this. Her berth had to be made up when the other berths were made up. All she could do was to

resolve that she would not go to sleep. Perhaps
she could jump up when the time came. But,
alas! before the time came, she was so far asleep
that she thought it was ironing day at Deacon
Spinley's, and each successive kitchybunk of each
twenty-foot rail that they passed over, appeared in
her dream as a flat-iron thrown by Mrs. Spinley at
the crash towel which was hanging on her roller.
So Jane did not " see Niagara " that time.

Forty miles east of Windsor everybody was
awake, and began to say he had not slept a wink
all night.   Jane had washed herself in a few
thimblefuls of cinder soup, which at her call
distilled like dew into the bottom of a cinder-
specked basin in the ladies' dressing-room. She had
rubbed some ring or lamp she had about her, and
those good genii, who were always her friends, had
arranged the " tangled dark-brown hair," so that
it seemed as if nothing had disturbed her.   The
same genii had created for her matchless and spot-
less cuffs and collars.   Then Jane went back to the
narrow quarters where she had slept, and found
that some other genii had been round with wands,
and that the berths had disappeared, and that in
their places were wide and deep " rep-covered "
seats, lighted by large plate-glass windows, through
which she could see, what was a sight quite new to
her, the blackened clearings, the log-cabins, and

the September harvest and fruitage of a new country. The sun was well up, and the scene was exciting enough, even to a person less hearty, healthy, and alive than Jane.

An hour of this rapid panorama shifting, and she knew, without question, that she was hungry. But Jane was a little reticent; and she lived on a principle which had never yet failed her, which the Western people embody in their direction, " Don't be first to squawk." Jane knew very well, that, by the same law of nature which made her hungry, Ned Bardles was already more hungry than she; and she knew that if he were in that condition, all powers in earth would be set in operation to meet his necessities, and, still more, that she should fare as well as he. So Jane still looked out upon pigs and stumps and corn and pumpkins and sheep and log-cabins; caught now and then the long, low line of the lake which they were skirting; saw in a few moments more that the number of cabins increased, and that they were approaching some place with a name; saw Ned Bardles begin to bustle, and to stir up the nurses and the children: and thus it happened that in fifteen minutes from the time when Jane was well aware that she was hungry, she was hustled upstairs in the steam ferry-boat at Windsor, had been placed opposite some sausages and fried oysters, by that most at-

tentive host who presides there, was receiving his
assurances that, every hand-bag, veil, umbrella,
newspaper, and shawl-strap were in such safety as
the bank of England even did not give its specie,
and was listening to his explanations of the length
of time which was before her for her meal. " Central Michigan! were they going by the Central?"
Heavens! what hours were before them then for
breakfast! In all which her voluble and hospitable friend was substantially correct. Jane had
time enough for a good breakfast.

The Bardles children, sandwiched in with nurses,
were at her left. At their extreme left they were
protected by Mrs. Bardles. Mr. Ned Bardles, belonging to a sex which has rights, was downstairs,
far from any breakfast-room, watching their baggage as it passed the customs-officer. So were all
the men of all the parties. The ladies and children,
therefore, were well forward with their breakfast,
— the children had finished their beefsteak and
omelet, their sausages and fried oysters, and
were beginning on their buckwheats and maple
sirup, when four gentlemen filed up from 'the
lower deck to take such chance of breakfast as they
might, and found seats opposite our friends. The
last of them flung his cap and gloves on a table,
ordered " coffee, steak, Indian bread," drew a stool
into place, and turned to sit opposite Jane. It

was Horace Vanzandt. One of the lucky double-sixes of travelling !.

A bright, hearty, pleasant addition he made to their party. He and Jane had not met now for more than a year, and only for a few moments then. All six of us suppose, looking back upon it, that neither of them appeared to the other as changed; certainly, neither would have said that the other was "improved;" still, as we have talked it over, our verdict has been, that these two fresh and true young people could not have knocked about in the world as much as they had in two years, more or less, since the famous Greyford sleigh-ride, without gaining that self-possession, information, tact, if you please; that facility in expression, and facility in listening, which varied society gives, to which the reading of good novels contributes, which, all combined, so lighten up man or woman in intercourse, even with the nearest of their old friends. At all events, Horace had a world of information about people in whom Jane was interested, which was new to her, and she as much that was new to him. Still more, he had been making rapid steps in his profession. He had learned very thoroughly, by this time, how little he knew; an immense acquisition for the youngster of three and twenty. She had moved, as people say, in the society of Boston and Newport; among people no

whit more intelligent or highly-bred than those she
left at Greyford, — but among people of many more
types, and their experience had varied hers, and
had quickened her methods of expression. So it
happened, if we six have rightly analyzed and syn-
thetized, that Horace was more quiet, more simple,
and far more profound in what he had to say; that
Jane was less shy, and more animated, in what she
had to say. Certainly, talk ranged over an immense
range ; but neither said any thing of the bear.

The Bardleses all made Horace feel at home.
Indeed, they were occupying almost the whole
of a drawing-room car with their immense party.
Nor is there a better chance for long and satisfac-
tory talk than in a good drawing-room car, when
the road is well ballasted, and the train well run.
No postman, nay, no door-bell, there ! So, for a
happy hundred and fifty miles, be the same more or
less, they talked, they amused the children, they
read the September " Old and New," they talked
again, and cut out cats and horses from paper for
the little ones, and talked again, and talked again ;
and so they came to Marshall, where the train
stopped for dinner. Dinner was soon over, and all
the party were back again in their car but Ned
Bardles himself, who was taking the last possible
moment with his cigar. His wife, as usual, began to
be uneasy ; the train began to start, when Ned

appeared at the door triumphant, threw it open, and waited on the platform for Nettie Sylva to come in !

Our readers may recollect the circumstances under which Horace Vanzandt and Nettie Sylva parted at the North Denmark sleigh-ride. We have tried to make them understand with how much and with how little feeling Nettie wrote to him when he was first in New York; how far she then felt hurt by his manner in writing to her, and how far she pretended to feel hurt. We have also tried to make the reader understand how deep was the wound which Jane Burgess had received, when, in face of the observations of the mild police of Greyford, and of every decision.of its common law, Jeff Fleming, who had been supposed to be hers, and hers only since they outspelled the best spellers in the district, had transferred his heart and hand to this same Nettie, after his long illness at the deacon's. To analyze and synthetize on those yearnings was comparatively easy. It is not quite so easy to say just what went through each heart of the three, and each mind, when they met so unexpectedly in the drawing-room car at Marshall.

They were all fond of each other ; that was certain. The girls were very fond of each other. Still, Jane did not think Nettie had ever treated

Horace fairly, and she had told her so more than
once.   For all that, in the very depth of her heart,
Jane was glad that, as things had turned, Nettie
had treated Horace as she had.   It was clear to
Jane's well-balanced mind that Nettie never could
have made Horace happy, and she doubted whether
Horace would have made her happy.   Now, to
pass to Nettie, the bright, pretty, coquettish thing
we must confess she was; she was "just as glad
as she could be" to see them both.   She said so,
and we all six think she was.   It was her way to
be glad; and she was more apt to be glad when
she was on the top crest of a wave that seemed
likely to topple right over, than on any conceivable
level of any summer sea.   Still, though Nettie was
"just as glad as she could be," she undoubtedly
was well aware that Jeff Fleming was as entirely
Jane's property, when he came frozen stiff into
the deacon's house, had only Jane asserted suze-
rainty, as was any unmarked log the deacon's
property when it was flung up by the river on his
meadow.   Nettie knew this in her guilty heart;
and she knew as well that that night when she had
played "*Les Larmes*" to Jeff, and he, susceptible,
tender fellow, had been so tearful, so tender, and
so happy, she knew, or thought she knew, she had
been giving a great wrench at Jane's heart-strings.
And as for Horace, — Horace had comforted him-

self with Rachel; yes, verily. Still Nettie did happen to notice that the guard-chain Horace wore was that she knit for him, and that there had been a time when she could have kept him in Greyford for ever had she chosen. So, though Nettie was "just as glad as she could be " to see them both, we all six think that it was with the joy of wild adventure, and that she was curious to know how many of the egg-shells among which they were all to tread would be broken, and how many would hold firm their yolks and their albumen.

It must be confessed that neither of the girls seemed externally in the least disturbed by any of these reflections; they kissed and laughed, and held each other by all four hands ; then Nettie did all the necessary civilities to Mrs. Bardles and the rest; and then the three, Jane, Nettie, and Horace, nestled down into one *vis-à-vis*, and began talking of how it had all fallen out that they had all come together. Horace was trying to persuade himself that he ought not to feel confused. Had not Nettie snubbed him, once, twice, thrice, n times? to take his favorite mathematical formulas. Nay, had she not accepted Jeff willingly, in defiance of him and of Jane both, and of all Greyford beside? None the less is it true, that, of the three, Horace was the only one who for a moment appeared to be ill at ease.

But this did not last long. They were soon telling each other facts, and facts are an immense relief
when there is any loose screw in people's sentiments. Nettie was explaining about her journey-
ings. Mr. Holley was prospecting in his eternal
lumber speculations, and had taken Rachel with
him. They had been up in Minnesota, beyond St.
Paul's, she knew not where. Nettie, meanwhile,
had been staying with an old friend at Ann Arbor.
She was to meet the Holleys at the Sherman House
in Chicago on this particular day, and here she was,
so far on her way. She had been riding with them
all the way from Ann Arbor without knowing it.

Then the Holleys would be in Chicago with
them all! And Mark was there already. What
fun!

Neither Jane nor Horace dared ask Nettie where
Jeff was. And Nettie, dashing as she was, did not
happen to tell.

Evening found them at Chicago. Horace was to
go to his quarters at Mrs. Worboise's. The Bardleses and Jane were all to go to the new house in
Erie Street. But all parties first went with Nettie to the Sherman House. There, sure enough,
they found Rachel Holley and her father. There,
as it happened, was Mark Hinsdale, making a
friendly call. The girls both thought that he and
Rachel seemed on a very brotherly and sisterly

footing. Five of the six, in the chances of life, had brought up at Chicago. They agreed they would all see the sights together the next day. Who could tell when they all should come together again!

CHAPTER XX.

THE sight-seeing lasted longer than they had expected; and all parties of our friends grew well wonted to Chicago before it was at an end. The Bardles *cortége* was settling down in their new house. Mr. Holley's combinations about the lumber lands in Minnesota seemed to draw out into longer and longer convolutions, which he explained to no one, and for which no one cared. They began on their lion-hunting with determined ardor, supposing that they must finish it in three days. But the days lengthened into weeks; and for every day of every week, these young people found themselves together almost every afternoon, every evening without exception, and sometimes in the morning. There was an excursion to Hyde Park, the pretty watering-place of Chicago; there was an excursion to Riverside, that wonderful and beautiful country town, where, before your house is built, your sidewalk is laid, your water and gas-pipes ready, your drainage adjusted; where in short, every grievance of ordinary building is cared for before you begin. There were the stock-yards to be seen, under the oversight of Mr. Denison, a new-made friend of Mark's, who was very attentive, and with whom that sad flirt Nettie made very rapid acquaintance. Always there was, for a place of rendezvous, the cool, pleasant reading-room of the Johnsonian Library, where Mark had created for the time a vat of lemonade, having ordered ice by the week from the ice-man. There were the elevators to be seen, and explained in detail by Horace. There were the water-works, with the most interesting and courteous explanations from Mr. Chesborough and Mr. Clarke. Jane, Nettie, and Rachel had all been teachers; and they had found some old Normal-School acquaintance in the high school, which had a great interest for them. And in Mr. Barry they had the most instructive and kind guide in the treasures, then still in their fulness, of the Chicago Historical Library. In those days there was a great deal for intelligent curiosity to see and enjoy in the young city of the Lakeside.

No one of them, perhaps, observed it then; but the rather unusual fact for them, that they were not precisely paired, brought these young people into a relation new to them, and much more fresh and healthy than they had ever been in before since childhood. As they had grown to be men and

women, they had always, by some fate outside
themselves, been thrown in couples. At the sleigh-
ride, for instance, already spoken of, it was to be
Mark and Rachel, Jeff and Jane, Horace and Nettie. In New York, it was Rachel and Horace. In
Boston, it was Jane and Mark. Always they had
been counted off by twos, as the drill sergeants
say, whether they would or no. But in these
various walks, rides, and sails of Chicago, that arrangement was necessarily broken. For there were
only two of the young men, — nobody knew where
Jeff Fleming was, — and there were all three of
the young women. It might well be that there
was some Mr. Denison, or Mr. Marsh, or Mr. Fay
beside, of the party, — very likely two or three of
the Chicago gentlemen, who had found out that
three pretty Yankee girls were seeing sights together. But the old doublet combination was
broken up. If they started in one arrangement
for a walk, they came back in another. And, without their thinking much of it, each of them was
thus making out the real life and character of the
others a thousand times better than they ever did
before. And no people can find more surprises in
each other than those who have seen each other
since they were babies.

Perhaps the only person dissatisfied with these
daily arrangements was the excellent Mrs. Wor-

boise, the only person who saw from the outside how these foolish little pawns were moving to and fro. Mrs. Worboise would get up nice, bountiful teas for the young people when they came home all alive with the excitement of walk or drive ; and she would watch at the door — oh, so earnestly ! — for their return. And when her dear Rachel came, a little earlier than the others, with some Mr. Fay, or Mr. Marsh, and not with Horace, Mrs. Worboise did not like it at all. And when, last of all, Horace came in with Jane Burgess, Mrs. Worboise did not like that at all. Mrs. Worboise had been sure that Horace and Rachel were meant for each other, ever since they went to the Cooper Institute together. And why he did not hold by Rachel, she did not see ! And why Rachel did not hold to him, she did not see ! She had almost a mind to speak to Rachel ! She could not bear it !

No ! dear Mrs. Worboise, no ! all the half-dozen of us think you had better not speak to Rachel. Speaking to them does no good, we think : we think it does harm. The truth was, that Rachel and Horace had helped each other, had helped each other a great, great deal. He had been kind to her, and she had been kind to him. In the loneliness of New York, this had been to each of them a great comfort. But comfort is not every thing. And it was made perfectly clear to Rachel's mind

in the days when they were in Chicago, that she
liked this merry Mr. Marsh, and this thoughtful
Mr. Fay, and this kind and attentive Mr. Denison,
just as well as she liked Horace. And Rachel was
quite too true to make Horace fancy that she liked
him any better. What Horace found out, perhaps
we shall some day know.

One Saturday night, as they landed from an excursion on the water, Mr. Forsyth, who handed
Jane on shore, and walked up the street with her,
asked her where she was to go to church the next
day; and, before the party separated, she held a
congress on the street-corner that they might arrange to go to church together the next day, on
their last Sunday in Chicago. On their other Sundays they had been broken up, by one and another
chance, and parted. This time they would go together.

To this they agreed; and, after a little chaffer,
it was determined that Mark and Horace should
meet at the Sherman House, escort Rachel and
Nettie to Mr. Bardles's house, where Jane should
be in waiting, and they would all go together to
Unity Church, on the North Side, to hear Robert
Collyer, who had not long returned from England;
and this they did accordingly.

They were not too late, certainly, but not too
early; were met by a courteous gentleman at the

door of the church, who found they would be glad
to sit near each other, and apologized that he must
therefore place them near the door. The church
was large, without galleries; it was already well
filled. The low pews, curving a little back in the
middle, were ranged so close to each other as to
give a social or congregate aspect to the congregation. And the first feeling with our Connecticut
friends was, that they were at home.

The organ was of sweet tone, and was very well
played; something almost weird in the voluntary
started the tears in Rachel's eyes. Then the
preacher rose in the pulpit. A large, strongly-
built man, with full, cheerful face, iron-gray hair,
and sympathetic, though piercing eyes, he read the
opening hymn, with a home-like earnestness, that,
in an instant, made them forget him, while they
were lost in the emotion of the lines. This direct ·
simplicity controlled them even more when he read
the Scripture. The passage was that in Luke, describing the unfruitful fig-tree, and the allusion to
the eighteen men who were killed by the tower in
Siloam. The young people felt almost as if the
eighteen were their own friends, and wondered
why they had never before cared for their destruc-
tion. After prayer, the congregation sat silent,
while a few plaintive chords from the organ seemed
to take up the eager and intensely personal peti-

tion. It was really a relief that no one said a word, for those overcharged minutes. And when the preacher rose again, with the hymn-book, and read the first verse of the hymn, with intense feeling, no one was surprised that he laid down the book, and sat down, as if he could read no more.

> "I want a principle within,
> Of jealous, godly fear;
> A sensibility to sin;
> A pain to find it near."

After the hymn was sung, he gave out his text.

" Or those eighteen, upon whom the tower in Siloam fell and slew them: think ye that they were sinners above all men that dwelt in Jerusalem ? "

Our young friends had never heard such a sermon. They were magnetized by the speaker's personal power; they were led along in perfect sympathy by his simplicity; they were moved to intense feeling by his undisguised emotion. In the beginning, this or that quaint illustration or suggestion, thrown in without any reserve in his curious Yorkshire dialect, made them turn to each other sometimes with a sympathetic smile. But, before he was done, sympathy expressed itself rather by pressure of hand with hand, or stillness even more rapt than ever. For he was speaking

now of the mutual and common life of men.
How impossible for any one of us to live for himself, or to die for himself! We must not say nor
think, that those are publicans, and we are purer
than they: do they sin, is it not because the
atmosphere of their lives has been so tainted?
and who is responsible for that atmosphere, if
not we, among the rest? He alluded to the
horrible frauds detected just then in the New
York Ring, but it was without invective; from
that allusion he passed on to speak with intense
feeling of that average conscience of the nation, in
which the conception or execution of such frauds
could be possible; and he held man, woman, and
child to the duty of purifying that conscience,
and quickening the common life. The whole
hushed assembly testified by its subdued manner,
as the service ended, to the power of this personal
appeal.

As our friends began their walk home, Nettie
found herself walking with Mark Hinsdale. "If
I lived within twenty miles of that man," she
said, "I would hear no other preacher. I would
come here if I came barefoot. O Mark! what
lives we lead! How can one fling away life as
one does, when, as he says, the thoughtless make
others thoughtless and the brave make others
brave?"

It seemed to Mark that he had never seen the real side of Nettie, beneath her merry play, before.

Jane and Rachel were together, Horace with them. "I was never in a Unitarian church before," said Rachel. "Are they always so grave and silent as they leave church, and as they go home?"

"I doubt if they always hear such sermons," said Horace. "These people seem to me to feel as I do; as if I never knew before my duty to the world, or as if"—and he paused and shuddered—"as if we were all on the edge of a common calamity."

CHAPTER XXI.

A S the five went and came on that October Sunday, how many times they said to each other, what they had said so many times before: "If only Jeff Fleming were here, it would be perfect!"

In saying this they were wholly wrong. The truth was, that, if Jeff Fleming had been there, they would, almost of course, have paired off in one of the old and familiar combinations. They would have lost just that vivacity of the new discoveries which they were making all the time; and making precisely because their partnerships changed with every new house into which they entered, and, indeed, with every other change of their little plans.

Meanwhile, Jeff was coming to them, though they did not know it, a good deal faster than the old poetical expressions for full speed can tell. He was coming a good deal faster than the average wind comes. He was coming as fast as high-pressure steam, thrown first on one end and then

9*

on the other of the pistons of a first-class engine
from the Boston Locomotive Shop would carry
him.   Now, if any of the new school of poets
wants to write a realistic poem about Jeff Fleming,
let him try putting that statement into rhythm,
verse, and rhyme.

After he has done this, he may go on to say,
that a little after they left Cass Corners, on that
October Sunday afternoon, three or four very wild
cows, tormented by five or six wilder German boys,
left the pasture where they would fain have been
quiet, broke through its fence, and were rushing
across the railway, when the express, to which
Jeff had intrusted himself, struck full on the
whitest of the herd.   She disappeared ; but the
engine was not so fortunate with the other cows,
and when it was done with them, it was lying in
the prairie, some feet below the level it had been
running on, gasping the last inarticulate word
which it would speak for many days.   Jeff and
the other passengers, startled from their naps,
sprang up, to discover that they were not hurt,
and to call an unexpected town meeting for the
advice and assistance of the conductor and engineer.   The hours spent in contemplating the
wrecks of engine and cows, in repairing damages,
and in waiting for another engine, threw them
wholly out of time.   The road was no longer

theirs, to take the expressive phrase of the craft. Their pride was humbled, as is a great cardinal's after his fall. Only this morning, and every thing got out of their way! Only this evening, and they must shirk off upon sidings, and get out of everybody's else way; all because four cows did not understand the eternal etiquettes, and know that precedence. must be given to an express-train.

So was it that, as Jeff and his companions at last struck Lake Michigan, and thought now that all was clear for them to approach Chicago, it was already well advanced toward midnight. Some one, who stepped in from a way station, bade Jeff look out and see the prairie fire at the northward.

Prairie fire, indeed! One passenger after another threw up his window on each side of the car, and looked into the night air; and as they rushed northward, at their old speed again now, and the flames and glowing smoke-clouds grew higher on the horizon, every one knew that this was no fire of hay and straw and stubble, but that the city itself, which was home to most of them and harbor to all of them, was in flames.

They dashed into the station, wild for news, to find all silent there. The throng which usually welcomes the arrival of an express was elsewhere now; not one hackman to urge his claims, not one teamster to plead for a trunk. Even the few women who found themselves on that Sunday train, saw that their friends had not come to meet them. The porters and switch-tenders on duty could hardly tell them more than what they knew already, — that Chicago was in flames.

Few indeed had stopped to ask this, only those who were strangers as completely as Jeff Fleming was. The larger part had leaped from the car platforms as soon as the motion was slow enough, and had disappeared at once on their way to warehouse or to home, which they knew must be in danger. Jeff himself, who knew not the name of a street, and indeed had no special place to go to, as soon as he found that he could learn nothing from the porters, rushed, self-directed, toward the line of fire. At first the stillness and solitude were terrible to him. All was light as day, and yet desert as midnight. He could hear his own boot-heel on the sidewalk, and in that square he could see no one. But, in a moment more, when he was in the presence of the fire itself, he saw why there had been solitude before. For now he had come into a jam of people, who did know the city, as he did not, and were on one of the great ganglions of its circulation. Jeff felt a terrible pang cross him, as he saw the struggles and horrors of this crowd. Here was a young man, with a sick

child of four or five years old in his arms. Oh,
how wretched her pale face was! "Will you
make way for me? this child is dying." And the
poor mother was close behind. Jeff felt it like a
personal pang cross him. Where were the three
Greyford girls in this wild confusion? Were they
lost in the crowd, as he was? Was there any
one to take care of them? Point by point Jeff
crossed that street. Between the back wheels of
wagons there is a little space, even in a terrible
crowd, of which a resolute pedestrian can avail himself. And Jeff was not a man to shrink. He
crossed the avenue, — pressing still towards the
fire — ran up a street which was almost desolate
again, and this time faced a coffle of horses, wild
with fright, — some of them hooded in the jackets
of the men who had led them from their stable,
others, blindfolded by such rags as could be seized
upon, — haltered together, and flanked by as many
men and boys as could be brought into the service,
driven from the light, down into safer regions,
where they could be harnessed in their turn, and
put to the work which was so essential. Jeff
shrunk into a doorway till this wild *cortége* passed
on, and then started again for the line of fire. He
came on it in a moment, sooner than he expected,
— came close on a steam fire-engine, whose foreman, hoarse and black, was just giving the orders

to limber up, that she might be put in a station to
windward.   Jeff saw by the unconscious gestures
of the men, that the flames, or the burning brands,
had leaped over their heads as they worked; he
could see that the treacherous eaves of a high
warehouse forty rods behind them were in flames.
Jeff had found his place now: he bore a hand manfully with the rest, at the tongue of the engine;
neither questioned why, nor made reply, as one
order after another was given; only admired the
sublime audacity of the foreman, who was doing
his personal duty still, and doing it cheerfully, in
the face of such tremendous odds. " Easy with
her! Away with her! Softly, boys; steady.
Here we are ! " — as she wheeled round into position, — as, in a miraculously short time, a line of
hose was run out, — as a spirited fellow carried it
up half the height of the guilty warehouse, — and,
amid the cheers of the few workmen, drenched
back the spiteful flame, and then turned his fountain on the roof opposite.   Short-lived triumph,
indeed!   They had not been three minutes in position, sending out hose, hither and thither, to points
which seemed assailable, when, as Jeff rose from
his knees, where, in a deluge of water, he had been
coupling two bits of leading-hose together, he saw,
what the foreman did not see, so eager was he
in his attack, — another Mansard roof, a whole

square to windward of them, all bannered and pen-
noned in flame. Jeff simply pointed it to the
foreman, who nodded in reply with a grim, hard
smile, called in his hose once more, coiled it
roughly as he might; once more gave the order he
had given so often, — "Limber up, boys! No
good here! Easy with her! Walk her along,"
— and directed the new station. It was as if they
had been spitting at the flame.

Jeff was willing to work, but not at such work
as this. It was the foreman's duty, very good for
the foreman; but it was not his. And, as Jeff
saw the steamer in position once more, he ran up,
he knew not why, toward the Court-house, which
they had seen towering high in the distance. He
left the line of fire for the moment, called by voices
in the crowd which had gathered in the lighted
square, and turned to join them. "Take hold,
gentlemen; take hold! Do you mean to have
these poor fellows roasted alive?" These were
the first words that came to Jeff in the midst of
the uproar; and, in a moment, he saw the position.
There had been a theory that the Court-house was
fire-proof. Now, the basement of the Court-house
was used as the county jail, and was filled with
prisoners. The keepers, doubtful as to their right
to release them, had gone to whoever had that
right, for some sort of sign-manual. Meanwhile,

the cupola of the Court-house was in flames; the
heat and horror of the fire made themselves known
within stone-walls below. And this army of
wretches, whose separate cells had all been un-
locked by the retiring wardens, was screaming
within for freedom; while the strong outer doors
were bolted and locked. They were all shut up
together, in one undistinguished crowd. The cry
of oath and entreaty could be distinctly heard by
the smaller crowd outside. But, in that smaller
crowd, some man of sense had understood the
exigency, and had voted himself into command.
The workmen who were relaying the pavement
of the square had left, on Saturday, a convenient
timber with which they adjusted its grade. "Take
hold, gentlemen; take hold! Do you mean to
have them roasted alive?" The sovereigns who
were passing understood the exigency, and rushed,
at this command, to the rescue. Jeff seized the
timber with the rest, — thirty, forty of them had
hold of it together. "Back! back! a few steps
back! Now! One, two, three!" And they rushed
at the gate, to be well-nigh overthrown by the
recoil. "Once more, men! back! a little back!
Now! Are you ready? One, two, three!" And
once more their hands were torn, and they thrown
back on each other, as the gate refused to yield.
But their cheerful leader, after examining its con-

dition, reported favorably of the effect. "Don't give it up, men. Back again!—little more!— little more! Now! One, two, three!" And with rather more skill, and a swing rather more elastic, they rushed again at the gate, and this time it was certain that something inside had given way. An answering cheer from within. Some swings of the battering-ram, directed with more precision, if with less force, and then, in one instant, the gate swung away, Jeff knew not where; and one black stream of life poured out from the gateway, into the street, with howls and cheers and gladsome oaths, and scattered to be seen no more. Jeff stood still, almost wondering why no one spoke in articulate words, and, in a moment, found himself alone. He was the only man who had nowhere to go.

Then recurred to him the question which had come to him so often since the young man passed him with the sick child, — "Where are the Greyford girls?" Where, indeed? and how was one to go in search of them? I have had just such a question put itself to me in a dream, when, all of a sudden, it appeared that some one who should have been there was not there. Was it a little strange, that Jeff's question did not first frame itself into, "Where is Nettie?" though he had a provoking letter from Nettie lying next his heart,

N

and had been wondering how he and she were to
meet each other, and whether he were jealous of
the Mr. Marsh or the Mr. Denison she had been
writing about? No: the spontaneous question
was distinctly, not of one, but of all: "Where
are the Greyford girls?" Jane Burgess, whom
all Greyford had voted to be his; Nettie, who had
said that by all that was holy she was his; and
"poor Rachel," as Jeff always called Rachel
Holley. Jeff felt that if he could see them, or
help them, that was what he was dumped down in
Chicago at this moment for; not to be serving
ejectment warrants on rascals, or dragging steamers out of the way of the flames.

Where were the Greyford girls? Asking himself this question, he rushed into the throng
again; hoping against hope that some fatality
would answer.

Where were the Greyford girls? They were
not together.

At that moment of time, if a somewhat defec-
tive chronology can be relied upon, Jane Burgess
was startled from an uneasy dream, which need
not be described in a story which has to do with
realities more terrible than visions. Ned Bardles
was pounding at her door. "Jane! Jane! there's
a great fire! Sophy is nervous, and you had

better get up and dress yourself; it will comfort her." By such weak devices does the less confident sex attempt, in times of peril, to give courage to the stronger. Not that Ned Bardles's courage or confidence gave way all that day, or till this time. To this hour, he thinks that if a particular Irishman had thrown a particular bucket of water where he, Ned Bardles, directed, half Chicago would have been saved that day; and his own house, with the rest, would have stood sure. Jane started up. Sure enough, the light was flaring through her window, and she could see every picture in her room. Sensible Jane! She had the wit at that moment to know which frock would be best to work in, and that if her getting up were for any good, it was for work. Sensible Jane! Frock, shoes, hair, every thing, was in order for work, when Ned Bardles next dashed up the stairway. She flung open her door, and asked what she was to do.

Still Ned prophesied smooth things. His wife was packing some trunks. Perhaps Jane would feel more easy if she were ready for a sudden removal. For himself, he was at that moment fastening the step-ladder which led to the roof. If Jane would come up in a minute, the roof was flat at the very top, he knew her head was steady, she would like to see the show.

"See the show, indeed?" Jane's packing was finished right soon; and, with her own hands, she dragged her heavy trunks into the passage, and down the stairway, to the front hall. Then she ran up and joined Ned on his lookout.

Beauty and terror! Such beauty and such terror! The howl of the flames, the rush of the tempest by her, which made Jane fear to step outside upon the roof, and made her beg Ned not to step so recklessly from side to side; the leaps from point to point, now of burning brands, as one called them, for want of a better name, now of columns of flame, which seemed to move wholly without law, or defied law; and above all, the heavy canopy of smoke and flame, white below, night-black above; and with its whirls between, lighted or shaded with every conceivable glare or cloud of white, of yellow, of orange, of scarlet, of crimson, of purple; the gamut of fire, here harmonized, there raging in discord; the voice of power and the spectacle of power hushed Jane at first, she did not know whether in terror or wonder. Then she cried, "Ned! come down, come down! You can do nothing here; come down for the children. Take them somewhere where they will be safe!"

But Ned declared, as he supposed with great calmness, though Jane could detect the quickness

of his speech, that it was idle to run away from a
fire which was a quarter of a mile away. If she
would notice the way the wind was blowing, she
would see that it had already passed them. Unless the wind changed its direction, they must be
safe. Still, if Jane chose, she might have the
children up and dressed, if she thought Sophy
would feel easier. As if the children hadn't been
all dressed, to their India-rubbers, long before!
Ned showed her the buckets which he and his
neighbors had been arranging on the roof. He
had already wetted every spout; and indeed,
even in the heat in which they stood, that whole
range of roof-tops looked as if it had been drenched
with a sudden shower. But even Ned's voluble
eloquence was checked when Michael's voice, from
the foot of the attic stairs, announced that the
water had stopped running. This was a call that
did summon Ned from his commanding station,
and sent him downstairs, to find what faucet had
been turned wrong. Alas! it was a faucet that
Ned even could not set right. In one fatal zig-zag
from the spot where it was born, the conflagration
had dashed across the city to the roof of the great
water-works, which seemed so far away. That
roof had fallen upon those engines which the moment before represented the maximum of human
power, as they also, like Jeff and Jane, were

working their willing utmost in their great duty. And so they were still.

But the indomitable Ned Bardles would not quail. "It isn't as if we hadn't got the reservoir." Again he conferred with his neighbors, laid off his working parties for the stairways, draped his out-houses with carpets and bockings, rolled a hogshead here, and another there, invoking all the traditions of early New-England life, and, as the night waned, filled them, to be in readiness for the crisis. No one within the range of Ned's line of battle could escape the contagion of his energy.

But, for once at least, the doubtful wife was the better prophet. She was preparing for retreat, while Ned was preparing for fight. Does such a union, perhaps, make the true general? She compelled Michael to harness the horses into the light wagon which stood in the stable, and bring it round to the door. What did not she and the children pile into that wagon! Her father's portrait, and Ned's mother's; the basket of silver-plate, which had been carried upstairs when they went to bed; two or three of those trunks of hasty packing; nay, on the floor of the little cart, in the midst of all these accumulations, stood sublime the easy-chair into which Ned had always liked to fling himself, when he came home tired, at

night, from the office. The wagon stood there,
hour after hour; and from child to grandmother,
when any one lighted on any thing in the house
which seemed particularly precious, it would be
carried down, and by some mystery crowded into
this wagon. And still Ned said it was nonsense;
that the fire had passed them, and there need be
no fear.

None the less did the last come. From a little
reconnoitring tour, he came rushing back; with
his own hands flung little Carl upon the seat in
the wagon, called his wife and the others out,
bade Michael mount and take the reins, lifted
Retty upon Michael's knees, and bade him drive
slowly to the base-ball ground. Sophy and Jane
and the little procession followed, arms filled with
little household gods. Ned Bardles himself went
back into his library, swung round his neck his little travelling-bag, looked his last upon his happy
home, locked the front door, put the key in his
pocket, and followed the retreat.

He overtook Sophy in a moment. "Wilmarth's
house is gone. They were not out of it two
minutes before it was gutted. All that square is
gone. I tell you, Sophy, it isn't like flame: it is a
wall of fire, sweeping down, and nothing stands
against it."

"Thank God, the children are all safe!" said

Sophy. And brave children they were. They hugged their little treasures tightly, and stamped along in firm order, at their aunt's or their mother's side.

A short relief at the lake-side. Michael unloaded his wagon, and they made there their little bivouac. "At least, we are safe here, where there is nothing that can burn." Retty and Carl grow used to the situation, stop asking questions, and begin to see which can throw stones farthest into the lake. And then, in one instant, with one more change in the eddy of the wind, there is a column of black smoke down upon us, from some pile of pitchy lumber, and Ned has Carl in his arms, and Sophy has clutched up Retty, and Jane is dragging John, as Michael leads the way; thick, pitchy darkness in this smoke, though we know the sun has risen. Michael leads us through by-paths well known to him. "This way, Miss Jane! Jump down here, Mrs. Bardles! I have the boy, ma'am." Turning this way, turning that way; a mud-scow here, a raft of floating lumber there; now a fight with a drunken boatman, now running across a tottering plank bridge, which has been left for us, by some one fleeing just before us, and we are safe again.

Arrived on the deck of a crowded steamer, Ned Bardles eagerly calls his roll, — "Retty, John, Carl, grandmamma. Thank God, we are all here!"

And then the captain of the boat called to them, to say that he must put off into the lake; that any who preferred to stay on land must go on shore. A tempest on the lake, and this storm of fire on the land! There were but few who did not prefer the chances of going to the bottom, to enduring longer trial of the battle on the shore.

Ned Bardles determined to stay, with his children. He gave Mike his choice, whether to stay or to go; and Mike said, — the faithful fellow, — " As ye 're all safe here, there may be some one else that needs me. I think I 'll go and see. "

There is the answer to Jeff Fleming's question, so far as one of the Greyford girls was concerned; and she, be it said in passing, the one whom the public opinion of Greyford had assigned to him as his own property, until Nettie Sylva had turned his susceptible heart in another direction. No great likelihood that Jeff Fleming will find Jane Burgess on that storm-tossed steamer in the offing. Perhaps he will, — stranger things have happened in this story. But we will see.

It was indeed one of the peculiar horrors of the great fire, that, in the flights and rescues, there were so many different tides of human life, sweeping in different directions at the same moment of terror, and each parted from the others. The

10

fugitives who fled to the lake were parted from
those who had escaped southward, and, yet again,
beyond that first line of fire, which swept across
the North Side, there was a third army of the
houseless, whose flight was northward; an army
enlarged as every new block gave way. In a
thousand instances, the fathers of families had, in
the night, left their homes, apparently secure, and
gone down town to work for the safety of their
property; so that, when the crisis of flight came
for wives and children, they were parted from
those who were used to care for them, and on
whom they were used to rely. For after the tunnel was rendered useless, and the bridges gave
away, the North and South Sides were completely
parted from each other. It happened, as in a
thousand other cases of those who were - closely
tied in life, that the little party of our friends was
so broken, that their history must be followed, not
on one only of the lines of retreat, but upon each
in turn.

Where were the Greyford girls?

As for Rachel Holley, at the moment when Jane
and Sophy and the children fled from the house in
Erie Street, after a night of anxiety, Rachel Holley
was comfortably asleep in bed, wholly ignorant, of
course, that half the town was in flames. After a
day at the Sherman House, Mr. Holley had brought

Rachel down to Mrs. Worboise's, well out of town on the South Side; and that good woman was only too glad to welcome so dear a friend as Rachel in her new quarters. Horace was there too; and, in the sight-seeing of the Greyford party, they had had many a merry rendezvous and jolly tea-drinking at these hospitable quarters. The alarm of fire Sunday night had kept Horace out; and when Rachel went to bed, he had not returned. The family at home had looked at the fire from the window before going to bed, but they were quite too far from the scene of it to be disturbed by the noise of the alarm. Good Mrs. Worboise slept too soundly to be careful whether her "boarders" returned at one hour of the night or another. Indeed, when she woke, with her maids, to start things in the morning, it was some little time, as she said afterwards, before she looked out of the window. She looked then toward the south; and she had been stirring "nigh half an hour, zif 't was any other day," before she knew that there was not a man in her house, and that, a mile away, half the city was in ruins. So was it that Rachel slept on. It need hardly be said, that, as soon as Mrs. Worboise got any information, she communicated it to Rachel, and the other ladies of the family.

Horace had walked home with Mark Hinsdale on

Sunday evening from the Sherman House, where
Nettie Sylva and her father still remained. Mark's
home was well out on the West Side, as has been
said. The young men were talking together of
Horace's plans, when an alarm of fire was given,
and, not long after, they could distinctly see the
light; of which both of them spoke with some
anxiety, so critical had been the fire of the night
before, of which they had, just then, been examining the ruins, and so tremendous was this
tempest which they had both been facing as they
crossed the town. Neither of these young men
had that divine instinct for running to " a fire "
which is a characteristic of most young Americans.
But in a tempest like this, after such an experience
as last night's, an alarm of fire in De Koven Street
was no trifle; and, without pause, each of them
arrayed himself for work, and Mark gave notice to
his landlady that he had his key, and she need not
sit up for him. Far to windward as they were, he
had of course no fear for her house; and he was
right. But, as a little hose-carriage rattled along
and passed the young men, both of them spoke
with anxiety of the means of fighting the enemy;
and Horace recalled with a shudder his words of
the morning, — " as if we all were on the edge of
a common calamity."

They came to work, and they had enough of it

before they were done. Not with the engines.
There was little that they could do there. Till
midnight, and after midnight indeed, the plucky
little steam fire-engines were thumping away with
precision and power; the water-works were deliv-
ering deluges of water; and for the hauling the
machines to and fro, the volunteer crowd that runs
with the machine gave all the help that the firemen themselves required, "dead-beat" though
many of them were by the work of the night before. But there was plenty of work for two intelligent young fellows with heads on their shoulders.
They ran first to find Fay, at the counting-room
of his lumber-yard. Fay was not there, — no one
was yet there. But it was so clear that that whole
yard would be in the range of flame within ten
minutes, that Horace did not hesitate to enter the
counting-room through a window, open the outer
door with a crowbar, and then pile into an express-
wagon, which Mark had brought to the spot, the
desks of the two partners; indeed, every thing
movable they could find. The safe they would
have taken too, but it was clearly too much for
the cart. This was in the early hours, when to
hire an express-wagon was still a possibility. Mark
sent the whole in triumph up to his own lodgings,
just as Mr. Vanderlacken, the senior clerk, appeared. Fortunately, he had the keys to the safe;

and he and the young men made short work in emptying that, and carrying the contents to places supposed to be places of security. That sort of sudden work, of new exigency and new provision, rapid determination and action as rapid, made the history of the night. It all changed, of course, as well in range as in the feeling with which they worked, after the fire leaped across the river, when all men who were awake knew that there was now a question as to the existence of the town.

The Chicago River is a sluggish little stream, formed by the union of two streams about half a mile back from the lake. After the union, the one river flows eastward into the lake, or did, till the canal changed its current. The two streams, before they meet, flow, one north, one south, to the point of union. The West Side, so called, is west of them. Several bridges and a tunnel unite it with the North Side and the South Side. These, in turn, are separated from each other by the river, and united with each other again by bridges and a tunnel. The rivers, or river, make the harbor of the city. To one who rattles over the bridges in a carriage, they seem narrow as ditches. But when you see two steamers pass each other, or when you see a steamer turned round in the stream, you see that there is more width than you supposed. The fire having begun on the

West Side, our friends had supposed that its havoc would at the least be checked by the river; bad enough, indeed, that it should only be checked there. No little part of their service of that night had been on board vessels, which seemed to be in the line of fire as the terrible tempest drove it on. It was, Mark thought, a little after midnight, when, as they were recrossing the bridge, from one of many expeditions to what then seemed a region of safety, they paused a moment to look northward, and first felt that their confidence in the river also was a delusion. They could see then how the storm, which seemed higher than ever, was flinging fire-brands upon the poor lumber-sloops in the river; nay, once and again a burning brand would soar, as if devils were carrying it, quite across the stream. With the thought of what might, nay, must happen, if the fire got lodgement on the other side, Mark and Horace at the same moment began to think of other duty than carrying account books to a place of safety. "Do you believe they know of this in Erie Street?" said Horace, thinking of Jane. And Mark confessed that he had been anxious to go and see if they were not frightened. While they questioned, a sharp flash sprang up, a very column of flame, on the leeward shore of the river. A moment more, and a hose-carriage came rushing across the bridge, and they heard the firemen clearing the way for the steamer. "Run up to Bardles's," said Mark. "I will go round by the library, and, if all is safe there, I will join you."

So Horace crossed back, and found his way to the Lasalle-street tunnel; but he was not to come to Erie Street so easily. First a loyal effort to help on her way an Irish woman and three children; then an adventure with some terrified horses, who were led out from one of the North-side stables, delayed him longer than he knew. He promised to take — and did take — one of these wild horses to a private stable as far up as North Avenue, where it was thought he would be safe; he mounted the terrified creature bareback, as he had done more good-natured beasts in old Greyford days. But when he returned from this knight-errantry he found the line of fire had crossed to the lake, and that he was cut off by it from Erie Street. If, as was perhaps possible, he could have crossed there, he did not rightly find his way. He chose in preference the Indiana-street bridge; and, though more anxious than ever about Jane and her friends, he thought his best way to reach them was to return to the West Side, and so pass round the west of the fire. He had not any fear, even then, of the Sherman House and Nettie Sylva. But he had thus undertaken a long journey; and it was, as any one will see who knows the ground, journey long enough to account for his failing to arrive at Erie Street before Jane and her party fled.

Nettie and her father, meanwhile, who had gone to bed early at the Sherman House, were not in the absolute security which both Mark and Horace imagined. As early as one o'clock they were up and dressed. The nervous and careful doctor himself carried their trunks downstairs. He had bidden Nettie put on her hat and walking-dress, and she was all ready to follow him. Every one assured the doctor that he was rather rushing into harm's way than away from it; but he had the feeling that he should surely be safe with some old Greyford friends well up on Lasalle Street. With another gentleman, he secured one of the heavy coaches of the house, and with their own hands they piled on their trunks, and piled in the ladies of their party. So swiftly was the movement carried through, that in ten minutes the whole party were safe at the hospitable house on Lasalle Street, which the doctor had selected as " so much safer than a hotel."

Alas for poor human foresight! The doctor had run just in the line of the tempest and of danger.

Not his party alone, but perhaps twenty other people, had gathered in the house. A pile of

10*   o

trunks, sheet-bundles of clothes, and other rescued property, encumbered the sidewalk. Everybody was made welcome, but meanwhile everybody was uneasy. The ladies and gentlemen of the house were engaged in bringing out valuables, and their guests in packing them, when, pop! the gas stopped, and every one knew that the gas-works had gone. Not that they needed such light much. The light in the sky left few houses dark, as that morning crept along from midnight to sunrise. The work went on, and none too fast. One of the gentlemen had just succeeded in securing a furniture-wagon, when the scout at the corner of the square rushed in, crying that it was really the last moment; that every woman must be gone; and under Mrs. Goodhue's lead, the long *cortége*, arms heaped full, took up the line of march for a house in Dearborn Street. The gentlemen promised that they would bring the trunks where they would be all right. And so, with less difficulty than might have been expected, all came safe to Dearborn Street, and again all met a cordial welcome, to have just the same experience again as a few hours passed by. Almost the same words describe it. Nettie had long since cast loose from any property of her own. She had gallantly taken charge of a little portrait of Mrs. Goodhue's mother, — which was itself a large lift for Nettie

to grapple with, — and of a travelling-bag of
Mr. Fontenelle's, which, as she knew, contained
a hundred and five thousand dollars in five-
twenty bonds. Nettie had declared to Mrs.
Goodhue, that the portrait should be as safe
as the lucre. At the Gracies' house, she had
worked as faithfully as the best. But when the
order for flight came again, she embraced the picture, and, by science known to herself, kept the
big bag hanging on three of those little fingers, —
" they were strong, if they were so small," as Mag-
gie Mitchell says, — and again they started for
some place known to Mrs. Gracie, which was " certainly protected." But the streets were more encumbered here. Nettie got confused, or some one
else got confused. She could not cross Clark
Street when she would nor where she would; and
when she was across, a great torrent of black smoke
compelled her to stop a moment; and then she
could not see one of the party. What strange
creatures New-England girls are ! The first thought
to Nettie — little laughing flirt, as you think her,
dear reader — was, that on Friday only, she had
been sitting in the High School with her friend
Miss White, and had heard a bright girl read
from the second Æneid, how Creusa acted when
she found herself in just the same scrape in
Troy.

"For while we seek the by-ways as we run,
 Careful the more frequented streets to shun,
 My wife, Creusa, in the darkness blind,
 Torn by some wretched fate, is left behind.
 Perhaps she lost the narrow path I found ;
 Perhaps she fell, exhausted, on the ground.
 I looked not back, nor thought to look until
 We reached the ancient shrine on Ceres' Hill."

But our friend Nettie had no thought, however, of " going under ; " her only anxiety was about Mrs. Goodhue's picture ; which, after all she had said, she would have died for. She rushed on bravely with the throng, and was thrown for a moment against the shafts of a wagon, so that the young man at the horse's head apologized to her. Nettie smiled as she thanked him ; and he recognized her, though she did not know him. Her pretty face was black with smoke and dust. The tears, forced by the smoke, were running helplessly in white channels down her rounded cheeks. There was but one attention which, in that crisis, the gentleman could pay her ; and he paid it. " Miss Sylva, would you like to have me wipe your eyes ? "

" Thank you," said Nettie, as merrily as she had said " Thank you " when he took her down to supper the Wednesday evening before. And this true knight, — whose name will ever be unknown, — with his one disengaged hand, drew a handkerchief from his pocket, and wiped the precious tear-drops from the prettiest eyes in Chicago. Who wills may make a sonnet of that tale! Nettie thanked him again, and laughed heartily again. He laughed as well, — offered to take her parcels, but she declined, — and she forged on her way, and he on his.

Where she went, she did not and does not know. Why she went, she hardly knew. Only, at last, she was all wrong. She came into an empty street; that must be wrong! Still she hurried through it, to see that, right and left, as the square ended, she was blocked by fire, or by smoke which she dared not pass. Back by the way she came! " Yes: this is right. This is the broken elm-tree I noticed. But, no! it is not right. I never saw that hogshead in the road. God help me! What is right? That smoke is too thick to charge. Back here? No! that is all too far gone. Could I have crossed back, and found Clark Street? Ought I not to have held by the wagon?" Still, she did not surrender the picture. No! nor did she lose her head. The loneliness was the worst. How she got there, she did not know. And clearly, that street was wholly abandoned. · At that instant, one puff of wind revealed to her the retreating line of wagons, on one of the northward avenues. Only a moment;

but enough for Nettie. She sprang into the smoke cloud, holding her breath, and, with her eyes shut, plunged on, running as fast as she could run with the picture. She smelt such smoke as she never smelt before, but she tried not to breathe. Nor was this in vain; forty paces of such running was enough. The air cleared; she was within twenty paces now of the wagons; one rush more, and then the picture-frame struck on some corner of a fence, and Nettie fell, helpless, and for one instant senseless on the ground.

———

Meanwhile, Mark had found the Johnsonian Library in very different plight from what he expected. Some fatal shaft had lighted early on a wheelwright's shop, just opposite that institution; and, at the moment of Mark's arrival, this shop was in flames. What a pity he had let Horace leave him! for by this time there were few enough volunteers to be recruited in the work of carrying out MSS., medals, and such other treasures as Mark knew were most valuable of all; or to take them to shelter, if in this storm of fire there were shelter. It was still early in the morning; but the people who were out and at work, were at work too eagerly for their own affairs to pay much heed to medals or to manuscripts. Neither for love nor for money could Mark find wagoner to help him, in the little range through which he dared to try. Ready money, indeed, he had none; having carefully left his watch and pocket-book at home when he and Horace started; and that night credit was worthless. Two or three light handcarts and a wheelbarrow he did impress. He and two of the trustees, white-headed old clergymen, and Miss Baylies, the assistant in the school hard by, did yeoman's work with these in the little time they had. But this was little enough; for, within an hour after Mark's appearance, the gutters of the Johnsonian had caught the flames, the little scuttle on the roof was on fire, and, in half an hour more, Mark and his trustees were driven, beaten, from the field. A stately carriage with a span of smooth, high-bred horses, was piled full of the manuscripts and medals; and trustee number one, mounting the box himself, drove it triumphantly from the ruin. Mark and the other trustees, and little Miss Baylies sought other fields of duty.

No question where Mark would go. "Where are the Greyford girls?" had been his question, even when he lay out on the Johnsonian roof with a hand-hose, when he descended into the Johnsonian crypts with a lantern. Now that he was free, he could find out where they were, and this was his first thought. Of course, the intelligent reader thinks he will go for Jane. Did he not write to Jane those beautiful sonnets? Were not his letters to her, all the summer, so personal? Yes; and yet he did not go for Jane. Perhaps he thought Jane well balanced enough to care for herself. Perhaps he thought that that part of Erie Street was in less danger than the Sherman House; or perhaps he pretended he thought this, and really, in his heart, felt that if any harm came to Nettie Sylva, he should never forgive himself; that if Nettie were lost in this chaos, his life would not be worth living. For my part, I think this storm of fire revealed a great many people to themselves. I think there was a great deal of time, while people were on the roofs of houses, or sitting in the night-air under the sky, when they learned a great deal that nothing else could have taught them. Of this I am sure: that when Mark Hinsdale saw that the Johnsonian was one mass of ruin, he rushed to the Sherman House by the shortest route he could find open. He never once thought of Rachel Holley, whom all Greyford thought he ought to think of; he did not think, more than a moment, of Jane Burgess, who had been kind to him and good to him; he thought of Nettie Sylva, because he knew her life was the other half of his life, — that if he could save her from suffering, that was what God had sent him into this world for; and, unless he could save her, it was not worth while for him to live.

He came to the Sherman House long hours after
Nettie had left it. It was standing, though so
much else around it was gone. Its white walls
were red with the reflected light. Mark could see
smoke starting from the roof, but the building
seemed unchanged. How little while since he had
left Dr. Sylva's pleasant parlor in the corner of
the fourth story! He rushed in. He was ordered
back, and had to obey. But orders went for little:
the house was well-nigh empty, for its fate was too
certain; and Mark was in again, and in the doctor's parlor. There was the copy of "Bret Harte"
on the table, which she had read from last night.
Mark seized it, and put it in his pocket. There
were the rosebuds Mrs. Hubbard had sent her.
Mark seized them. Could it be that any chance
had neglected her and the doctor? He tried
the doors from the parlor. The doctor's room
was empty. He knocked and knocked at the
other door. " Nettie! Nettie! " No answer. He
turned the key, — he rushed in, to meet a column
of smoke which blinded him. But Mark had tried
smoke before, that night. Down on his knees, he
crept across the room, and was right; for there
was a little space from which the smoke rose. He
held his breath till he pulled both pillows from the
bed. Certainly no one was there. But could he
find his way back to the door? He could not

stand. He could turn to the place where he thought it was, — but where it was not. The door was a wash-stand. " I shall be dead in ten seconds," said Mark to himself. But in five seconds he had crawled to the door, was in the parlor again, was in the draught of a broken window, and was safe.

He was downstairs again. A porter he found declared that Dr. Sylva went north: which was true. Now for a journey north! And how? This bridge is closed, that tunnel closed: — the way is cut here and blocked there. But Mark did it. Southward, westward, northward, eastward, he passed round the fire. And then among seventy-five thousand people, Mark was looking in every blackened face, to see if it were the doctor or Nettie. If he met any man he ever saw before, he asked for Dr. Sylva or for Nettie. He rushed down one square and another, till he met the line of fire. He crossed back and forward through every street which took the line of fugitives. Church after church he tried, where people had sought sanctuary. And so was it, that making a short cut, where he thought no one blocked the way, he saw a woman emerge from the smoke, heavily burdened, — he saw her trip, and fall upon the ground senseless. He ran to her, and lifted her gently, and wiped her hair from her face, and he knew he had Nettie Sylva in his arms!

It is a hard thing to keep up the chronology of such chaos as this, in which few men looked at their watches, and of which the chief time-marks are the moments when the water failed, when the gas-works gave out, and when the sun rose. We have still to tell what became of Horace Vanzandt, whom we left crossing Indiana-street bridge, westward, to look for Jane Burgess; who, as he hoped, was half a mile exactly behind him.

Slow work, indeed, flanking the sea of fire on that morning. But Horace was steady as he was impetuous. Still, long before he had worked round to the south side of the river, every bridge and every tunnel to the north side was impassable, and every man he questioned assured him that the part of Erie Street he was asking for had gone. None the less did Horace persevere. A ditch like that could be crossed, if he had to swim it! Swim it he did not; but he did bribe an Irish boatman to carry him across the mouth of the river, — and so pressed his way up on the lake shore. Nay, he came to the ball ground, had he known it, some two hours after Jane and the children had left it.

He stooped down and picked up a jumping-jack some child had dropped there. Surely he had seen the grimace on that painted face before!

It was madness to ask each fugitive if he had seen a party of ladies, with three small children. Madness or not, Horace asked and asked again, and received answers, now wild and now coherent. They sent him hither, sent him thither; but there was no Sophy Bardles and no Jane Burgess to be found by this questioning. Back he was beaten to the river-shore and the lake, by failure and by fire; and at last, unwillingly, after trying this scow and that schooner, was fain to take shelter himself on a little tug that was putting out to sea. Nor was he relieved here from the wretchedness that had surrounded him on the shore. Children without their mothers, mothers without their children, were piled together on the little deck. Water, of course, the lake provided them; but a little hard-tack, which was gone before night, was all the edible provision. And such a night! She lay at anchor in sight of the lurid, cruel fire. And how she rose and pitched in the gale. How would these wretched, half-clothed children live till morning? Still, we do live till morning. And then such wretchedness! "I am so hungry! Oh, dear; I am so hungry!" The captain at last pulled up his anchor, and ran down under the lee of one of the larger steamers. "For the love of Christ, can you give these babies something to eat?" And Jane Burgess threw down into the

tug one of the four loaves which Mike's fore-
thought had packed in the big basket which he
never abandoned. And Horace Vanzandt, little
guessing what angel answered his prayer, caught
the loaf, and, in a minute was dividing it among
these twenty starving little ones. A minute more,
and he had scrambled up the steamer's side. No!
It was not Jane he found. It was a sort of mate,
who could provide some blankets for the women
who seemed dying in the engineer's room of the
little tug below. Up and down, back and forth,
Horace passed on his work of mercy. And it was
not till he had seen everybody decently comfortable there, that he scrambled back upon the
steamer. He passed aft, where he saw a group of
children lying listlessly. He offered a little boy
the grinning jumping-jack. "Why, it is Carl's
jumping-jack! See here, mamma; here is Carl's
jumping-jack!"

And Horace turned, and Jane turned.

"Dear Horace!"

"My dearest Jane, is it you?"

Where are the Greyford girls?

For Jane and Nettie we have accounted. Let
us go back to Rachel, at good Mrs. Worboise's
boarding-house.

Rachel soon understood that she was on the

very edge of one of the greatest events in history, and was seeing it almost as little as if it had been in Moscow. She could, and did, run to the top of the house, and see a lurid canopy of smoke. She could and did make her way up, with Mr. Fay's assistance, against the current of fugitives, as far almost as Harrison Street, and saw something of the methods of the fight. But she saw the flight more than the fight; and Mrs. Worboise and Rachel, and all that household, instantly understood the emergency, and the duty next their hands.

"My dear child, this is sure: they will need something to eat, whatever else they need, or whatever else they save."

This was Mrs. Worboise's simple statement, founded on a profound philosophy. By "they," the good soul meant the human family in general.

Her washing-boilers were scalded out, — as if they needed it! — and as many hams put in as they would hold. With white arms and sturdy, she mixed self-raised biscuits, and plied that day her ovens. Open doors in that house that day long; no sign of flight. No man nor woman stopped to ask a question, but was asked to eat, and ate to the full. The water had given way; but Mrs. Worboise had a little " nigger boy," — as, in face of better light, she obstinately called him, — whom, by threats, bribes, and promises, she kept plying to the lake-shore for water; and her old New York filters did the rest. When she got a little ahead with her bread and ham, she devoted her attention to bedding. I dare not tell how many "shake-downs" she and Rachel and Mrs. Plinlimmon constructed on landings and floors. Mrs. Worboise could have hauled a steamer into action if she had been bidden; she could have sculled a scow, had she been bidden; she could have wiped a maiden's smoky tears, had she been bidden; she could have lain out on the roof of the Johnsonian, with a hand-hose, had she been bidden; she would have added emphasis to a battering-ram, driving in a prison-door, had she been bidden. As it happened, she was bidden to provide for a stream of faint and roving fugitives; and reverently and faithfully, hopefully and lovingly, she did that duty. Of course she did it well.

Whether it were morning or afternoon, I do not know; nor, I think, did any of the parties know. But, as the day passed, Mrs. Worboise, standing on the door-steps, saw the approach, on the street, of a long express-wagon, crowded with little girls, frightened and crying, or sometimes dumb and stolid with terror. She rushed down to ask where they were going.

" God knows ! " said Jeff Fleming who was on the high seat, carefully driving. " They are going wherever there is something to eat, and a bed for the poor things to lie in."

By the divine instinct of his healthy life, Jeff, who had sought vainly all day for the " Greyford girls," had lighted on these inmates of the orphan asylum.

" Why the little darlings ! " cried the good woman. " Bring them in — bring them in ! We are all ready for them here. Bring them in." And by this time Rachel and Mrs. Plinlimmon were at the tail of the wagon, and had each a child in her arms.

" Why, Mrs. Worboise ! who sent you here ? "

" Why, Mr. Fleming ! is it you ? "

So Jeff Fleming deposited his charge with Mrs. Worboise. A moment more, and a fellow sovereign stopped to ask for the use of the wagon ; and Jeff let him have it, on his promise to bring it back at nightfall. Jeff had hired it from he knew not who, for a hundred and fifty dollars down, on promise to return it next morning to he knew not where. Jeff had not tasted food since he left Cass Corners, twenty-four hours before ; and he was not sorry to smell Rachel's coffee, nor to cut into the good lady's ham.

" Dear Rachel," said he, after the rage of hunger was a little satisfied, and after each child was in bed in some improvised night-dress, "how much has passed since I saw you!"

.Yes, indeed! how much had passed! And as the afternoon waned, and as the evening gathered, and as they turned back from this or that corner, how they two were revealed to themselves and to each other! How honest and brave and true Jeff seemed to Rachel, though he could not expound science like Horace, nor talk sentiment like Mark. Of course, she did not say it to herself; but what a perfect rest it was to sit and talk with this hearty, simple, loyal friend, and not to be in terror of one of Horace's crotchets, or one of Mark's flights into the sky. The evening passed on. There was an alarm about a prairie fire southward. What a mercy Jeff was here! The tokens of rain came; and Jeff returned: all was well! And he? He kept wondering, as Rachel did, where Nettie was; and he hoped the Bardles family were safe; Nettie, to whom he was betrothed, indeed; and Jane, to whom he had been assigned. Still, he did not go again to look for Nettie. Rachel wondered why. Perhaps he knew better than Rachel did. Anyway, he was determined, that, if danger came that night to Rachel, he would not be far away.

Nine o'clock! Mr. Plinlimmon has come in.

11   P

They say it is all done. There are patrols on the streets. Gen. Sheridan is in command. The children are all asleep; but no one else wants to go to bed. Half-past nine. A carriage wheels to the door. A sharp ring and knock, and the door flies open. The parlor door, of course, flies open too, and Mark Hinsdale almost lifts Nettie into the room.

"Dear, dear Nettie! is it you? Lie right on the sofa here!" And Rachel is caring for Nettie with all the tenderness and sweetness of her own lovely life.

"And where did you come from, Jeff? Dear old fellow! how are you?" This from Mark, without one thought that this dear Nettie, whom all day long he had fought for, worked for, lived for, and almost died for, was supposed by everybody to belong to the "dear old fellow" who stood before him. Nor do I know that Jeff thought of it more than he. The day had taught Mark a great deal. It had taught Nettie a great deal. I believe Jeff had learned his lesson too.

How much they had to talk! There was every thing to tell. How much Mrs. Worboise made them drink! How much camphor she brought for Nettie's forehead, where the bruise was a bad one. How Nettie made them laugh! And then, again, how she made them cry! Mrs. Worboise could do nothing with them. It was Mrs. Plinlimmon who appeared at midnight, and sent them all to bed.

———

Tuesday morning they all slept late. No wonder. "Dear children," said Mrs. Worboise; "they shall have breakfast by themselves." And in a little back parlor they four met, late in the morning. Still so much to tell! Nettie knew she must have a private talk with Jeff: she must tell the honest fellow how wicked and how foolish she had been. And Jeff knew he must have a private talk with Nettie. He must tell her that he could not, in honor to her, marry her. But Nettie and Rachel came into the room together, as fresh and neat as if there had never been any fire. And Jeff and Mark were there before them, and could not ask either of them to go away. And it was not awkward, after all. "Jeff is so good-natured," said Nettie to herself. "He will not mind, and I can tell him by and by."

So they lingered over the breakfast, as surely no other four in Chicago lingered that morning, Did Mrs. Worboise guess? I do not know. I think she did. She loved Rachel with her heart's love. She loved Horace too; and yet, as she washed one little orphan after another, she said again and again, even aloud to the orphans, "She will do a hundred times better with that honest Jeff Fleming than she would ever do with Horace." And, though no one said this in the breakfast room, perhaps they all felt it too. And Nettie, guilty Nettie, pretty Nettie, flirting Nettie, — she had not gone through storm and fire without learning what she knew well enough before; only this time she knew it "perfect." She knew that such a treasure as the love and life of Mark Hinsdale was not a treasure to be fooled with, or thrown away.

No wonder that the coffee cooled, and the breakfast was long. But it ended. It ended when the door flew open, and Jane and Horace both rushed in. Jane all in tears, but handsomer than ever. Horace, tattered, worn, and dirty, but happier and prouder than he had ever been in his life.

He had had a chance to tell Jane how he had sought for her from midnight of Sunday till sunrise of Tuesday, — sought her with tears and with prayers.

And Jane had shown to him the one treasure she had saved from Erie Street. It was the little bear.

Had these young people trusted to the first propinquities, had they let the people of Greyford pair them, they would have trusted wrong: they would have lived for misery.

Had they trusted to the "propinquities" again, had they let the accidents of life pair them, they would have trusted wrong.

A terrible crisis tore away all veils, all etiquettes, all falsehoods. For once they trusted to the divine instincts of their own hearts; and they are happy for this life, and for ever.

Cambridge: Press of John Wilson & Son.

www.ingramcontent.com/pod-product-compliance
Lightning Source LLC
Chambersburg PA
CBHW030643030726

47497CB00006B/1923